SLOCU

With a hard jerk on the bits, he tried to control the upset horse spinning around under him.

"Easy. Easy . . ."

By the lake below, he saw the cause of the pony's upset. A huge grizzly reared up and roared at him.

He slid the Winchester out of the scabbard and levered a cartridge in the chamber. He turned Paint broadside, feeling the horse trembling under the saddle as he took aim. *Stand still for a second.* His finger squeezed off a shot at the galloping bruin. The bear, hit in the head, nosed down, pawing at his muzzle and issuing groans.

Round two to the grizzly's face made him raise his muzzle and give a last, loud moan . . .

DON'T MISS THESE
ALL-ACTION WESTERN SERIES
FROM THE BERKLEY PUBLISHING GROUP

THE GUNSMITH by J. R. Roberts
> Clint Adams was a legend among lawmen, outlaws, and ladies. They called him . . . the Gunsmith.

LONGARM by Tabor Evans
> The popular long-running series about Deputy U.S. Marshal Custis Long—his life, his loves, his fight for justice.

SLOCUM by Jake Logan
> Today's longest-running action Western. John Slocum rides a deadly trail of hot blood and cold steel.

BUSHWHACKERS by B. J. Lanagan
> An action-packed series by the creators of Longarm! The rousing adventures of the most brutal gang of cutthroats ever assembled—Quantrill's Raiders.

DIAMONDBACK by Guy Brewer
> Dex Yancey is Diamondback, a Southern gentleman turned con man when his brother cheats him out of the family fortune. Ladies love him. Gamblers hate him. But nobody pulls one over on Dex . . .

WILDGUN by Jack Hanson
> The blazing adventures of mountain man Will Barlow—from the creators of Longarm!

TEXAS TRACKER by Tom Calhoun
> J. T. Law: the most relentless—and dangerous—manhunter in all Texas. Where sheriffs and posses fail, he's the best man to bring in the most vicious outlaws—for a price.

Fc

JAKE LOGAN

SLOCUM AND THE BIG HORN TRAIL

JOVE BOOKS, NEW YORK

THE BERKLEY PUBLISHING GROUP
Published by the Penguin Group
Penguin Group (USA) Inc.
375 Hudson Street, New York, New York 10014, USA
Penguin Group (Canada), 90 Eglinton Avenue East, Suite 700, Toronto, Ontario M4P 2Y3, Canada
(a division of Pearson Penguin Canada Inc.)
Penguin Books Ltd., 80 Strand, London WC2R 0RL, England
Penguin Group Ireland, 25 St. Stephen's Green, Dublin 2, Ireland (a division of Penguin Books Ltd.)
Penguin Group (Australia), 250 Camberwell Road, Camberwell, Victoria 3124, Australia
(a division of Pearson Australia Group Pty. Ltd.)
Penguin Books India Pvt. Ltd., 11 Community Centre, Panchsheel Park, New Delhi—110 017, India
Penguin Group (NZ), 67 Apollo Drive, Rosedale, North Shore 0632, New Zealand
(a division of Pearson New Zealand Ltd.)
Penguin Books (South Africa) (Pty.) Ltd., 24 Sturdee Avenue, Rosebank, Johannesburg 2196,
South Africa

Penguin Books Ltd., Registered Offices: 80 Strand, London WC2R 0RL, England

This is a work of fiction. Names, characters, places, and incidents either are the product of the author's imagination or are used fictitiously, and any resemblance to actual persons, living or dead, business establishments, events, or locales is entirely coincidental.

SLOCUM AND THE BIG HORN TRAIL

A Jove Book / published by arrangement with the author

PRINTING HISTORY
Jove edition / March 2008

Copyright © 2008 by The Berkley Publishing Group.
Cover illustration by Sergio Giovine.

ISBN: 978-0-515-14426-0

JOVE®
Jove Books are published by The Berkley Publishing Group,
a division of Penguin Group (USA) Inc.,
375 Hudson Street, New York, New York 10014.
JOVE is a registered trademark of Penguin Group (USA) Inc.
The "J" design is a trademark belonging to Penguin Group (USA) Inc.

PRINTED IN THE UNITED STATES OF AMERICA

10 9 8 7 6 5 4 3 2 1

Prologue

He sat the bay horse back in the junipers, unseen, so he could study them sleek-brown naked Injun girls bathing in the crick. Couple of them didn't look half bad in the distance. He occasionally licked his sun-crusted lips, and the sharp edges of his whiskers scratched his tongue. Just watching them girls had the saliva flowing in his mouth like a flood. Way he figured it, he'd have him one of them hellcats picked out for his own before dark.

Just a damn shame that his pack mule Judy had kicked his last woman in the head. Blue Bell'd been what he called her. Took her three days to die. Damn hard for him to keep a good wife. Always something happening to them. That Arapaho gal, Antelope, got struck by a runaway wagon in Cross Creek and killed outright. Maybe he was jinxed or some witch had a hex on him. First chance he got, he'd have some fortune-teller see if it was true.

He wore a silver cross on a cord around his neck to keep the spirits away, but it might not be enough to ward off a real powerful spell caster. Had to be a reason that he was always breaking in a new woman. One got killed by Blackfeet who were raiding his camp for his whiskey. He couldn't recall her name. They bashed her head in with a stone ax. He kilt four of them over it. Revenged them pretty good for her. Ah, he remembered her handle—Puppy. Couldn't ever pronounce her real one. Looked like a brown-eyed puppy to him.

Time for him to get on with it. He shook loose his reata and made a loop. The Injun he wanted had long breasts that swung firmlike when she waded around. She was in the midst of them girls splashing and screaming at each other. Then, setting spurs to his pony, he busted out of the junipers and came swinging the rope over his head. Them girls seen him coming. They were big-eyed and looked shocked like surprised deer. Pounding that ole pony's ribs with his rowels and making the rope sing, he charged them. They began to scream and run like hell for the far bank. But the water was over knee-deep and that impeded their speed like he'd figured.

Bay hit that water, and he reached out with a hard toss of the reata. It went right over the gal's head and he jerked the slack hard, so the loop was around her shoulders. Didn't need to choke her to death. He dallied it around the big Mexican horn and turned Bay around. He glanced back as the gal set up fighting and screaming for her life. Too late now, gal. He'd done got her.

At the bank, he went to reeling her in out of the crick. She was struggling hard against his efforts, trying to brace her feet. When she was close enough, he reached down and jerked her up over his legs. Time to vamoose. He held her kicking, squalling, wet form over his lap and looked around. The others were already hiding in the timber, he felt certain—no signs of any bucks coming to their rescue. He set spurs to Bay and left.

Mighty fine package lying there soaking the wetness into his britches. He admired her shiny hard-looking butt and flailing shapely legs. He'd done good. He reined the hard-running Bay around some deadfall. He wanted lots of distance between him and her relatives by dark.

Sun was down when he picked up his two pack mules loaded with supplies. She'd continued to fight him like a wildcat, so he'd tied her hands and feet. Kind of like breaking a horse, you needed to get their attention. After that, things went smoother. He was high up in the mountains toward the pass when he decided to rest a few hours.

"We're stopping here for a while," he said to her. Didn't matter if she understood him or not. She'd figure things out soon. Besides, the night's air had begun to really get cool.

He eased her down, and she stood bound up, unable to do anything else. He stepped off his horse, jerked off a blanket roll from behind his cantle, and undid the leather ties. With a whip of it, the blanket unfurled and he draped it over her. He stepped aside and dug out his root to piss.

"That should keep you from freezing," he said when he finished—shaking and putting it away.

She never even nodded in the starlight.

He ignored her and began loosening cinches. No way, this close to them red devils, he'd unload the animals. If necessary, he could mount and ride for it. That completed and the animals hitched good, he dug in his saddlebags and produced some jerky. When he walked over to her, he held up a piece. She drew her head back.

"You'll get hungry," he promised her. Then he swept her up, blanket and all, and carried her to a grassy spot. There he set her on her butt, and then he re-covered her shoulders with the blanket. She never said a word.

Seated cross-legged on the ground facing her, he chewed on the tough jerky. She had lots of pride. Head up, chin out. He could see her high cheekbones underneath the large eyes that were narrow in the corners, giving her even in the half-light a hard, determined look. Nice boobs. They were long, firm, and the nipples pointed at the emerging stars overhead. Like a ripe watermelon, all she needed was plugging to see how she tasted.

He chuckled to himself over that. For the moment, he wanted to save that part of the honeymoon until he was in his own cabin. Besides, by then she'd know she belonged to him. Consenting sex always worked out better in the long run than raping her the first night. Dreamily, he thought about her in his arms—no way that nothing was going to ruin that night, he aimed to really enjoy it. Gave him a hard-on just sitting there and thinking about doing it.

He listened to a distant wolf. When he looked over at her, he saw by the quick look of discovery on her face that she'd heard the wolf too. Good. Wolves were feared critters, and that would make her want to be with him rather than run away. Keep up that howling, ole boy. This he-devil has him a new bride and you're going to drive her into his arms.

He laughed out loud. It was going to be a fine winter. Him and her up there and snowed in. Wouldn't be much to do save run some traps, bust firewood, and make love. The means for that was sitting less than four feet from him.

In the predawn glow, he undid her ropes and gave her some clothing. She quickly dressed in the frosty air, and this time she accepted some jerky. The leather leggings were a little too big, but she tied them off around her slim waist and put on the beaded and fringed blouse that came to her knees. Then she carefully wiped off the soles of her feet with her hand and put on the moccasins.

"You can ride belly-down or behind me," he said, using his hands at the saddle to indicate where she could sit.

She indicated in back of him.

"Fine," he said, and swung up. He reached down and she leaped when he lifted, so she slipped in place easily behind him. First time she had cooperated with him. He glanced back at her and nodded in approval. They still had a long ways to go. Two or three days hard pushing to reach his place.

When he spurred Bay, the two honking pack mules came on. Her arms flew around him and she clung tight. Her reaction caused a small grin in the corners of his unshaven face. Be one fine honeymoon they'd soon be having—damn, he could hardy wait.

Before noon, he crossed over the divide and saw no sign of pursuit from their lofty position. Stopped to stretch his legs and get his leather pants out of his crotch. She walked a short distance away to relieve herself. He looked over the wide expanse of treeless meadows that showed nothing but some scattered antelope and elk herds. When she came back, he caught her around the waist by surprise and swung her around.

"They ain't coming for you, darling, or they'd already been here," he whispered in her ear, and then he set her down. "Better get to moving, girl. We've got lots more ground to cover."

She never answered him or nodded her head, simply waited dutifully for him to mount. Then he hoisted her up behind him and they went on.

Day four, they were heading over the last pass. In the soft ground, he'd seen some days-old barefoot pony tracks that bothered him. What were Injuns doing in the Big Horns? Maybe a hunting party hoping to get a few fat elk before the animals rushed off the high country for the winter on the plains. Folks went to shooting at them, they got plumb cagey, best to get some of them before that happened. Still, as he looked at the snow-clad peaks above them, he knew that any Injuns in the Big Horns was bad news. They were all supposed to be on reservations over in South Dakota.

Cast-off breeds and renegades spelled trouble. They were cutthroats and thieves. Those sneaky bastards were always up to no good. He'd keep that in mind.

"We're about there," he said, facing the bright sunshine to check the time. Nightfall and he'd be jacking his old root in her till he wore out the hole. His laughter made him rock in the saddle as he rode.

"Yes, sirree, gal, you're going to become a real woman tonight." He reached down and patted her leg encased in buckskin. "Mighty fine one, I bet. Yes, sirree, you'll be mighty fine meat."

He reined Bay to the northwest. Trooper's Crick wasn't far across the high country. With his eyes half-squinted, he searched for any sign of them bucks. Nothing, not a dot even. He booted his horse on, jerking on the mule leads.

"We'll be home directly," he said more to the animals than to her.

At last, they were in the bowl between the timbered slopes

in the long meadow that led to his place. The sound of the water rushing out of the small lake above his cabin sounded like sweet music. His heart began to pound with excitement.

"There she is," he announced, and set Bay into a lope. He was going to bust her cherry before the sun set. With his right hand, he reached down and patted her leg as she clung tight to him from behind.

Bay snorted and shied sideways, about spilling them on the ground. But he caught the horn and they managed to stay on him. With a scowl at his horse, he reined him around. "What in the devil's got into you?"

The gal slipped to the ground and collected the mule leads, taking them toward the cabin while he fought with the upset pony. "What in hell's name is wrong with you?"

At last, he sent Bay toward the cabin in a hard run and passed the gal. There he dismounted, undid the girth, and took off the saddle, looking all around for the sight of anything that could be bothering his horse. Not a thing he could see. He would put hobbles on him. The mules would stay close.

She arrived and hitched them mules to the rack. He went inside the cabin. Needed airing out, he decided. It smelled pretty musty, like old socks. Best thing, it was intact and all his things he left there looked to be in place. Satisfied, he went out and carried in the heavy panniers of supplies she had uncovered. She was busy folding the tarp covers and gathering the ropes. He noticed she was neat enough for a squaw. Learned real fast. He started a fire in the small cook-stove and took two canvas buckets off the pegs.

"I'll go get us some water for coffee. Where that water comes off that lake is a waterfall. A shower, well, kinda cold, but nice." When she did not answer him, he shook his head in disgust. She must be deaf and dumb never to respond to nothing he said.

He set out up the hill, looking back. He saw the mules were already grazing near Bay. When he turned around, he heard a thunderous roar. A great cinnamon-colored grizzly was bearing down on him like a freight train. That was what the horse had smelt. He began waving the buckets like a wild man and cussing like a sailor. Stop him first, then confuse him. His heart was pounding so hard it hurt his chest. Step by step, he moved backward, facing the slowing bruin and putting on his show.

Ten feet from him, the bear raised up on his hind feet to let out a growl that froze his innards. He could see the yellow canine teeth, and slobbers flew from his mouth as ole grizz tossed his shaggy head from side to side. Something had him riled. Then he noticed the blood behind the grizzly's left front leg and an arrow sticking out of him. What dumb jack-ass had tried to kill a grizzly with a damn bow and arrow?

The horse prints. The barefoot ones. They were made by some stupid Indian boys out on a quest. By this time, the bear's powerful musk filled his nose. A strong male smell saturated in urine and bear shit. No wonder Bay had shied when he smelled it. Despite the frantic pail waving and shouting, the bear still advanced. Grizzly's roar deafened him as he continued to scream and frantically swing the pails. The cold realization that the bear was going to attack him ended when a sledgehammer blow from its paw struck the side of his head. Seconds later, he half-awoke on the ground, smelling the bad odors of the bear's breath and the sound of crunching bones. It was his own skull . . .

1

Slocum's ribs ached when he twisted in the saddle. Busted rib or two—the sharp pain caught his breath. He paused to look over the open country that was behind him before he went over the ridge and dropped down on the other side. No sign of those breeds. They'd be coming. He gave the paint horse his head and started off into the valley. In the distance, a small lake shone like a diamond in the midday sun. Hemmed in by the timbered sides, the green valley's carpet looked like a good place to let Paint fill his belly with grass and to let his sore-sided rider rest awhile.

He rode up to the edge of the water, and Paint drew back with a snort. He searched around with a frown. What had spooked Paint? Slocum could smell wood smoke, but saw no source of it. With a hard jerk on the bits, he tried to control the upset horse spinning around under him.

"Easy. Easy." He sent him off down the flat to try and get him over his fit. By the lake below, he saw the cause of the pony's upset. A huge grizzly reared up and roared at him.

He slid the Winchester out of the scabbard and levered a cartridge in the chamber. He turned Paint broadside, feeling the horse trembling under the saddle as he took aim. *Stand still for a second*. His finger squeezed off a shot at the galloping bruin. The bear, hit in the head, nosed down, pawing at his muzzle and issuing groans.

Round two to the grizzly's face made him raise his muzzle and give a last, loud moan. Then silence. Paint blew rollers out his nose. Shaking all over, he trembled, standing straddle-legged when Slocum stepped off him. Rifle reloaded, Slocum studied the pile of cinnamon-gold fur and a wave of relief washed over his tensed muscles. He had to be certain the bear was dead and not just stunned.

At the sight of movement to his left, with the rifle against his hip, he whirled, ready to fire. To his shock, a young Indian woman armed with a hunting knife came off the rise, and the roof of a small cabin could be seen behind her.

"That your pet?" he asked with a grin, indicating the grizzly.

"No," she said.

"Good," he said, acting relieved.

She pointed with her knife. "Bear killed him."

"Who's that?" He frowned, unable to see anything where she indicated.

"Never say his name. He kidnap me on Wind River."

"Oh," he said, taking a deep breath since the bear had not moved, except for his hind legs, which were jerking in the throes of death.

"You know him?" she demanded.

"No—I don't think so. I'll go look in a minute."

She spit in the direction of the dead man. "I am glad the bear killed him."

"Yes. I understand." He uncocked the rifle and put it on safety. With it back in the scabbard, he stepped in the stirrup, swung aboard, and reined the still-spooked Paint toward the victim. Giving the smelly carcass a wide berth, Paint looked warily sideways at the bear until they were by it. A hundred yards across the grassy ground, Slocum spotted the bloody mauled body. He dismounted and, with Paint grasping mouthfuls of grass, stepped over to the dead man. His bloody face did not look familiar. Maybe if he hadn't been so torn up— Slocum had to swallow hard to stand the obnoxious odors of the disemboweled body. He turned away from the horrible scene and met the brown eyes of the squaw, who'd walked up to join him.

"Is there a shovel?"

"Me get one."

"What is your name?"

"Easter. They call me that at mission school."

"Slocum's mine."

"You Bear Killer," she said with a sly look, and threw out her breasts under the beaded blouse. "No one mess with you. Big man kill big bear, huh?"

"Well, he's dead anyway."

Shaking her head, she took his arm and shook it. "No, you Bear Killer."

The pain drove him to his knees and he bent over grimacing.

"How I hurt you?" she asked with concern written in her brown eyes.

"Ribs are broken—"

"Come. I get your horse. I bury him later. Got whiskey for you."

She helped him up, then ran off to catch Paint and, leading him back, indicated the cabin. Slocum agreed, hugging his left side hard with his elbow.

"What hurt you?"

"Some men beat me up two days ago. I managed to get away from them, but they may come here looking for me." He paused to catch his breath, and she turned back to look at him.

"Maybe they end up dead like the grandfather bear." She nodded like that would be no problem for him.

"Where did you learn English?"

"Mission school."

He nodded and set out again for the low-walled cabin that appeared at the top of the rise. At the front door he could hear the waterfall coming off the lake. She was undoing his horse's girth when he turned back to her. Hurting too bad to assist her, he noted she soon had rope hobbles on Paint. With the saddle and pads in her arms, she came on the run.

"Go inside," she ordered.

He nodded and ducked under the lintel to enter. He put his hat on a peg and looked around. Cozy enough place. She loaded his saddle on a rack built in the wall.

"You sit on bed. I get whiskey."

He didn't need any more invite than that. His side felt kicked in, and he dropped his butt on the bed. She brought him a tin cup and small crock jug. He took the cup and she poured until he said, "Whoa."

She was maybe five-five or -six. Her raven-black hair was wrapped in beaded leather on both sides of her face with a beaded red headband. She looked at him out of round eyes that were slanted in the corners. She had high cheekbones. Her nose, once broken, was thin for an Indian, and her mouth was generous with a pouty, full lower lip. She was in her late teens with a willowy figure.

"Sit down." He indicated the army blanket beside him.

She did, and he took a sip of the whiskey. Tough stuff. It sure cut a path going down his throat. Even set his ears on fire—white lightning. He blinked and looked over at her.

"You want to go home?"

"No."

He frowned at her and turned back to try more of the painkiller. "Why not?"

"I am soiled. No one would want me."

"What's-his-name rape you?"

"No."

She leaned back with her hands on the bed behind her. Her proud breasts pushed against the deerskin over them. "Who would believe me? Huh, some old man might want me. He wouldn't care who I had slept with. So that he had a nurse, huh?"

"I guess so. You ever bound anyone up who had broken ribs?"

She scooted to the edge of the bed. "I can try."

"Good. We need some cloth. Wrap it around me and tie it off." He hoped that might give him some relief.

"Drink more whiskey. I find some."

He finished the liquor in the cup, and she brought some red cloth on a bolt. It would do fine, and they cut some off. He shed his shirt, wincing some, and when he finished that, she shoved another full cup in his hand. The whiskey was taking the edge off the pain, and he laughed when she wrapped him. But he gritted his teeth when she pulled the cloth tight and tied it off with all her might.

"How that?" she asked, leaning forward to look at him.

He nodded in approval, then downed some more firewater. In a moment, she was on her knees, easing off his boots. Then she swung him around by his feet so he was on the bed. She looked satisfied at her handiwork. "You sleep."

"I reckon I could, girl. Thanks," he said with a wince at the pain his movement caused.

Settled on his back, his discomfort eased some by the liquor, he closed his eyes, then realized he still wore his six-gun. He drew it out, placed it by his head, and fell off into a troubled sleep. There were nightmares that caused him to wake in a sweat. Smells of food cooking filled his nose, and he sat up on the edge of the bed in the candlelight.

She looked back and smiled at him. "Bear tracks coming."

"Good," he said, not thinking about the meaning. In his stocking feet, he stepped out into the cool night, realizing how good the stove heat had felt, emptied his bladder, and listened to the night sounds.

When he stepped back inside and closed the door, she brought him some golden brown doughnuts on a tin plate. Bear tracks—it came to him. The doughnuts were still hot, and he shuffled one back and forth in his fingers until he could take a bite. The sweetness and rich flavor made the saliva fill his mouth. He nodded in approval. "Very good."

"Have plenty bear grease to make them all winter," she announced.

Maybe she thought he'd be there that long. He ever got well enough, he'd leave Wyoming and head south for San Antonio. He could bask in the winter sun and make love to all the brown-skinned señoritas that he wanted. No snow, no cold, just dancing girls stomping to trumpet music on the patio. Twisting like vines as they performed to seduce him, and shaking their breasts as their heels clacked across the rock pavement. Ah, to San Antonio. No wonder Davy Crockett gave his life for the place.

"You have a woman?" she asked, busy frying more bear tracks.

He shook his head. "I have no place for a woman on that paint horse."

"You could stay here."

"I need to be in Texas."

"I think you lie to me. What is in Texas?"

He rubbed his palms on his britches. "San Antonio. Sunshine. No snow."

She wrinkled her nose and turned back to her frying. "I bet they don't have bear grease or bear tracks."

"Why do they call it Bexar County then?"

She laughed until it turned to giggles and bent her over. "You lie faster than I can think."

Carefully, she set her batch out to drain and took the kettle off the stove. Still amused, she crossed the room and stood before him. "I have never been with a man. But I would be with you, Bear Killer. If I am not to return to my people, then I wish you to show me the way."

He wanted to say he was too sore. He wanted to say lots of things to her. But he nodded and mumbled. "I am honored."

"Good," she said, and stripped off the blouse over her head. "I have washed the smell of him off me for you. The water was very cold."

"He's buried?"

"Yes, and the bear is skinned. I will render the rest of the grease later." She undid the waist strings and shed the pants. "A few hours ago, I thought I would be his woman forever. Now he is buried where two of his wives sleep."

Slocum shook his head. "How did you get the bear's hide off?"

"I used your horse to pull him over."

That impressed Slocum. Paint wouldn't get close to the bear's stinking mass for *him*. He rose and took his shirt and pants off as she drew back the blankets and scrambled onto the bed. The red-yellow flare of the candles shone on her smooth copper skin as she adjusted herself on the bed.

As he went down beside her, he realized he ached in many places. Should he save this until he felt better? No.

"Why did they beat you up?" She lay on her side facing him.

"I hate for anyone to use a quirt on a woman. One of them was whipping her with one. I told him to stop. Him and his friends jumped me, and they thought I was dead when they got through. I wasn't, so I stole their money and left them."

"Stole their money?"

"They'd robbed some stages. It wasn't much. Eighty dollars. But I figured that served them right for beating me up."

She laughed and eased herself closer. "Will this hurt you too much?"

It might, but he shook his head, fondling her long firm breasts. If he only felt better. But when he tried to rise, he discovered he couldn't—

"I see you are too sore?"

"Yes." He lay back in relief and the cold chills ran through his body. *My Gawd, what a baby I've become.*

He closed his eyes and passed off into sleep.

When he half-awoke, he found her naked form curled to him and her arm thrown over him. Felt good. He went back to sleep. When he woke again, she was gone and the bed beside him felt cold enough to know she had been up for some time.

When he stepped out to piss, he found her bent over a large kettle. She rushed over and hugged his waist. "You don't have to go to Ontonio today, do you?"

He laughed. "I couldn't if I wanted to. No, I will stay with you for some time."

"Good." She smiled, pleased, and rushed back to stir her rendering fat.

He stood at the side of the cabin, pissing a great steaming stream. He'd hate to have to ride anywhere today. Besides, this hardworking woman wouldn't be easy to leave. He could see she even had the bearskin stretched out with stakes driven in the ground.

"Where did you bathe?" he asked.

"At the falls."

"Oh." He shivered at the thought. "I bet that was cold."

"I will do it today. Who wants a woman stinks like a bear?"

"No one. Did this man ever say his name?"

She shook her head. "I never said a word to him. I was so mad at him for taking me from my people. I acted like I never heard him. His horse's name is Bay. 'Whoa, Bay, gaw-damn you.'"

He laughed at her mimicking the man.

"He said I was a watermelon and he would plug me."

Amused, Slocum shook his head. "But not till you got here, huh?"

"Yes, and he went for water to make coffee and the bear got him."

"Well, he picked out a winner. Figure he watched you very long to know that?"

She shrugged. "I only saw him coming on that horse and swinging that rope. I prayed to God for him to not catch me."

"I bet you prayed."

"Maybe God wanted me to come up here."

"Maybe he did. But we must be watchful. Red Dog, Snake, and Tar Boy may be on my trail. Run for cover when they come. They're mean men."

"I will watch for them. Day and night."

Good. He studied the high cloud shield. Snow or rain was coming in a few days. That would cover his trail, but they had plenty of time until then to find him. He hobbled back inside on his stocking feet. Hurt too bad for him to pull on his boots. Maybe she would put them on for him later.

He'd sure hate being caught by them in his stocking feet.

2

Red Dog took a drink out of the neck of the bottle and shoved the Indian girl Mia at the bed. "Get undressed."

Where were Snake and Tar Boy? He'd sent them after that fella who rode in on the paint. They should have found him and cut his throat by this time. Sumbitch stole his money. He dropped his pants and grasped his throbbing dick. Time to burn her leather. Damn, someone just rode up. Who in the hell could that be? He pulled up his pants. "Get under the cover. We got someone here."

Stupid bitch just lay there on her back with her knees apart. He shook his head, buckling his belt. Uncomfortable with his hard-on, he grabbed the six-gun out of his holster and went to the front door.

"Open up in there."

The voice wasn't familiar. Sounded like the law. He used his left hand to undo the bar with the pistol cocked and ready in the right hand. When he cracked the door, a man in a tan coat hit the door with his shoulder, spilling Red Dog backward. Red Dog fell firing his .44 at the intruder. The man's own pistol shot went into the floor. Black gunpowder smoke filled the room with a stinking sulfurous haze.

Red Dog crawled outside on his hands and knees and coughed his guts up. Retching vomit, he tried to see through his blurred vision if there was anyone else around. His pistol was still in his hand. Nothing moved but the intruder's sorrel horse, who raised his head with his mouth full of grass. When it went back to grazing, Red Dog uncocked the Colt. A sure sign there was no one else close.

Naked, Mia leaped over the body in the doorway and ran several yards past him before turning back to stand with her hands pressed to her face in fear.

"You kill him. You kill him."

"Shut up," Red Dog said, wiping his sour-tasting mouth on the back of his hand. "Who is he?"

"Law—man."

That was all he needed, a dead lawman on his hands. One damn fella steals all his money, and next he shoots a lawman. Holy Christmas, this was a mess.

"Get to packing, we've got to get the hell out of here." He rose to his feet and reholstered the pistol. What did this man have on him?

He turned the body over and dragged him by the boots out of the doorway. Wide-eyed, Mia went around the corpse and rushed on inside. Down on his knees, Red Dog unpinned the silver badge. It was worth something. Inside the coat, he found the man's wallet, and grinned at the sight of the folding money. He tucked it in his vest pocket. He looked at the bullet hole in the man's chest that had burned his shirt around the entry place. Crimson blood had stained the white material. Dog rose and pulled off the man's boots. Nothing need be wasted. Besides, this bastard would never miss 'em—he was stone dead.

"You know him?" he shouted to the squaw, who was cramming things in the canvas pannier like the place was on fire.

She shook her head.

"Damn dumb bitch." Scowling at her, he bent over, undid the man's suspenders and the gun belt so he could shuck the pants off the corpse. Lots depended on how important the man was—that could affect how hard the law would look for his killers. When he got the things he wanted off the body, he'd make damn sure they never found it. He struggled while pulling on the pants legs, but the britches at last came off.

Out of breath after sawing off the victim's ring finger with his big knife to get the gold band, he noted when the sorrel jerked its head up and look hard to the east. "Aw, shit." He dropped the knife and his hand went to the butt of his own handgun. Someone else was coming.

When he saw the familiar black hat and coffee-colored face of Tar Boy riding the dun pony, he let his guard down again. They better have gotten his money back from that worthless thief and cut his throat from ear to ear. Then two eagle feathers twisting in the wind on the unblocked hat of Snake appeared, and the man came on his white stud horse. Both men reined up short, staring hard at the body in the flannel underwear on the ground.

"That be him?" Tar Boy asked, rocking in the saddle with his hand on the horn.

Red Dog cut his eyes around to glare at the black man. "No, he's the damn law." He dug the badge out of his pocket and flashed it at him. "You two find that peckerwood stole the money?"

Tar Boy shook his head and dropped heavy from the saddle. "We done lost his tracks way down in Wyoming."

"You two go get drunk or something?"

"Naw, we done been in the saddle all this time. His track, dey's went up like smoke."

Snake spit off to the side and, looking sour-faced over the whole business they'd been on, the breed nodded to emphasize the black man's words. Then he pinched his own nose, leaned over, and blew a stream of snot out of his nostrils. "Sumbitch gone."

"Aw, I should of sent some kids to track him. We've got to get rid of this body and that horse and get the hell out of here."

"Where we going?" Tar Boy asked with a frown.

"Wyoming for now. Help her load that stuff on some packhorses."

"Yes, sirree. I go get some. Mighty fine saddle on that red hoss," he said, getting on his own.

"Riding a dead man's horse and saddle can get you hung."

Tar Boy stopped with his dun half turned away. "Still a mighty fine saddle."

"Go get them ponies. We need to get our asses out of here."

The black man agreed and set out for the ponies. Snake coughed up a hocker and spit it on the ground. Then, without a word, he rode off after Tar Boy.

Them two were getting worse. He ought to leave the three of them there for the posse that came looking for this dead man. 'Course Red Dog couldn't read and the badge's words meant nothing to him—so he didn't worry about the lawman's importance. Besides, in another hour they'd be shuck of this place. He laughed to himself. That damn farmer's throat had been easy to cut—those two snotty-nosed kids the same. Said they'd feed him outside that shack when he asked them for food. They didn't want no dirty breed in their house—no, sir. But he always wondered what had happened to the pretty woman in the tintype they had on the table. She must've died or never came out there with them.

"Come help me," he shouted at the squaw. Them pigs would eat the corpse in half a day. They were real hungry. He'd heard them squealing all morning long for something to eat. *Your dinner's right here*.

She acted upset, taking the man's feet, but she did her part. Carrying the torso, he forced her to go backward downhill to the pen. The pigs were really cutting up seeing them coming. A few even reared up on the split rail making a terrible racket. Dog and the squaw stopped parallel to the fence and on the count of three, they heaved the body over to the pigs. They wasted little time fighting over it and set in to seriously gnawing on the corpse.

Good. In a short while no one would know the man's identity. That horse, though, would be a dead giveaway. Red Dog would take it out of the country with them.

She carried the cross-buck packsaddles outside and piled them in the sunshine. Then she brought out the pads. He could see the other two driving the horses up there. Take five head to carry all their junk, food, and bedding. He wished they'd hurry. This place had begun to make the back of his neck itch. He regretted that damn Tom White getting away too. They'd probably never find him, and for sure Dog's money would be spent if they did find him after all this time anyway.

In an hour, they were loaded and gone. Dog led them off the ridge toward the Little Big Horn River and Wyoming. Mia rode the dead man's sorrel horse and acted like she was some kinda princess. Princess, his ass—she needed some more beatings so she knew damn good and well she was just some ole squaw for him to screw. He had lots to catch up on too. He looked back and watched Tar Boy, with a rifle in his arm, bringing up the rear of the packhorses.

Long past dark, they stopped and camped by a small spring-fed stream. They were in Crow country, but he'd kill a Crow as easy as he killed that dumb lawman. How did that badge toter know he was hiding out there? When Mia had the dishes washed, he caught her by the scruff of the neck, bent her over a pannier full of stuff, and threw her dress up over her back so her butt shone in the firelight. He dropped his pants while standing behind her, and took his hard shaft in his fist and guided it between her legs.

"Better put it in or I'll jab it to you," he said to her.

Her hand obeyed, and the head of his dick slipped in her pussy. When he hunched his dick hard into her, she grunted.

"I'm going to give you what for, girl. You been showing off all day on that damn red horse, You ain't nothing—" He grasped her hips and shoved his rod deeper into her. "I'll teach your show-off ass what you are."

He began to pump her harder and harder. With his hand squeezing her neck, he bent her farther over the pannier, and went faster trying to get his rocks off. "You little bitch."

His dick hurt. He needed to come, but it was like he had a piss hard-on and nothing could get out. He strained and strained but nothing happened.

Finally, he pulled the throbbing tool out of her and with a handful of her hair in his fist, he held her up to his face. "You put a hex on me?"

"No," she managed, inches from his angry face.

"Then suck on it and hard." He forced her on her knees and stuck it in her small mouth.

She worked furiously on it with her lips and tongue until he felt the charge coming up from his balls. Then he clutched a fistful of her hair, held her against his belly so she'd get it all. He came big-time and laughed aloud at her. She was about to gag when he pulled his dick out of her lips. With his thumb and forefinger, he grasped her nose between them, squeezed it shut tight, and forced her to swallow all of it.

Then he laughed. "That'll suit you right, you bitch. Go get my whiskey." He shoved her off her knees onto the ground with his boot.

"Where's that damn fella now that stopped me from whipping you? Huh?" he said after her.

"I don't know." She cowered defensively on the ground.

Using his finger for a pistol, he waved it at her. "If I ever learn you fucked him, I'll scalp you down there." He pointed at her crotch. "Hear me?"

"Me no. Me no."

"You'll think 'me no.' "

Dog glanced over at Tar Boy sucking on his cob pipe and sitting on his haunches across the dying fire. "Did she screw that bastard?"

"Naw, she be you woman. She don't mess around wid nobody." Tar Boy shook his head.

Hanging back to be beyond Dog's range, she held out the crock jug toward him. "Whiskey."

He snatched the crock and jerked out the cork. Then, looking mean-eyed at her, he took a swig and laughed. "Here, you drink some."

She shook her head.

"I said take a drink."

She reached out and had to use both hands to tip it up to her mouth. When she swallowed, she coughed and tears flew out of her eyes. Some liquor ran down her chin, and she wiped at it with the back of her hand. Then she blinked her wet eyes and under his demanding gaze took another big swig.

He took the jug back and bragged to Tar Boy, "I'm getting her warmed up, huh?"

"They always tell me liquor's quicker." The black man took out his pipe and laughed.

"Here, squaw, take another swig." Red Dog moved loose-jointed toward her, swinging the jug at her.

This time she took it without any refusal and turned it up. A smile crept into the corners of his mouth. When he took it back, he put his arm on her shoulder and led her to his bedroll.

"Get undressed," he said, and she began to obey. Untying the skirt and dropping it, she pulled the buckskin blouse off over her head. He took another drink, then handed the jug to her to hold while he undressed. She giggled and raised it to her mouth.

When she finished, he put the jug down and they crawled under the blanket. He pushed her legs apart and moved between them. Limber as she was, she'd spread her legs wide enough apart. This way, he'd get his root plumb up inside of her. Braced above her, he punched it in and began to pump it to her.

Her fingernails dug in his forearms and the electricity ran up his spine. He really went to humping it to her, and she raised her butt off the blankets to accept all of him. With her short legs wrapped around his middle, she was on fire with her butt off the pallet. She was rubbing her belly against his and the walls inside her had begun to contract, so he was really plunging hard with each drive to make his way back in her.

Soon, her claws were raking his back and he was mad with rage. Harder—faster, deeper—then he exploded and they fell in a pile.

He fell asleep still connected to her.

It was the middle of the night when Tar Boy shook him. "We's got company."

"How many?" he hissed, getting on his knees in the darkness.

"I figure it's a posse. They's up dere. Talking about it."

"Where's Snake?" He tried to see around in the pale light.

"Who knows where that breed sleeps?"

"Where's she?" he asked in a loud whisper.

"Done already gone to get us hosses. We's better grab what we can and ride."

"You're right," Red Dog said, putting on his boots with trembling hands. "Go. Go on, I'm coming."

"Sure."

Then he heard that war cry on the hill above them. He knew it was Snake. That breed was driving horses too.

"Hey, they're stealing our horses," someone on the ridge shouted, and shots popped in the night.

Dog took no time to see or hear anything else. He was running over the rough ground and through the box elder for the horses with one goal—to get the hell out of there. More shots and cussing behind his back, but he knew that that damn breed had given them a good head start.

He took the lead rope from the squaw and leaped on his horse. When he had his horse under control, she'd bellied up on the sorrel and was waving for him to go on. He did.

Sumbitches would get all his food and stuff, saddles, pack-saddles, and horses. Hell, he'd steal some more. He forced the horse to go faster.

3

Slocum's left side was still sore. After Easter's breakfast of flapjacks and chokecherry juice, she saddled his horse for him so he could ride up and check out the high country for any sign of Red Dog and his bunch. There was a bite in the north wind and a gray-goose sky when he hugged her with his good arm and kissed her hard on the mouth.

She put the back of her hand to her mouth and her eyes sparkled at the discovery. "That a kiss?"

"Yeah," he said, and made two attempts to swing into the saddle. Pain ran up his backside when he did make it into the seat, and he straightened his back with a nod. "That's for saddling my horse."

A devilish wink, and she smiled at him, giggling. "I saddle him every day."

"You've got a deal, girl." He put spurs to the tail-switching Paint, and left in a short lope for the ridge to the east.

He wore a jumper, but it hardly stopped the north wind's chill. He'd need something thicker if he stayed in the mountains. Paint picked his way up the slope in cat hops, and a pair of elk on the rim looked hard at him before trotting away. No time for hunting. Slocum needed to know if those renegades had been tracking him.

At last on the rim, he used the field glasses to scope the

open high country. He dismounted wth a catch of pain that made his lips close tight. At last, the pain let up and he let the gelding graze on the short grass. With a jack pine to lean his back against, he detected some smoke. Probably a small campfire at a good distance to the east. One puff was all he saw—enough to make him curious if it was Dog and his bunch or not.

Satisfied that that was the only sign, he remounted and rode in that direction, keeping under the hogbacks where he would be out of easy sight. He left Paint hitched in a grove of lodgepoles, and slipped to the crest so he could peer down into the next canyon, which he could see was the source of the smoke.

A silver stream ran through the narrow bottoms. His glasses set, he sat on his butt and scoped the cooking fire and the two Indians sitting at it. Then a third one showed up. They were only Sioux boys, he could tell by their dress and looks. They weren't Red Dog's bunch. But they were sure a long ways from their South Dakota reservation—must be on their quest. He hoped they wouldn't want his scalp.

Relieved they weren't the renegades tracking him, but still on his guard, he went back for Paint. With the glasses stowed in the saddlebags, he held his breath, remounted, and rode back toward the cabin without another single discovery besides a black sow bear and her cub cutting across open country in a high lope headed north. After she looked back at him, they both left in double time. He laughed at her and the clumsy young'un trying to keep up. A good horse in open country couldn't catch them, but they didn't look all that fast or graceful. Be time soon for her to den up for the winter. He reined Paint for home, huddled under his jumper with daydreams of the warm San Antonio sun and some snappy Spanish ladies clacking heels on a flagstone patio.

In camp, he found Easter busy pouring the rendered bear grease into skin containers to save for later use. She looked up and waved the loose hair from her face. "I found some pemmican."

"Good, we may need it."

She agreed, and put her hands on her hips. "It is cold enough to keep meat, but this bear meat stinks. We need a moose."

"We better kill some deer until my ribs heal some more. A moose is too big for me to move in the shape I'm in."

"Good." She stepped in, elbowed him aside, and took over when he fumbled one-handed with the latigos. "Go inside, there is hot coffee."

"I saw three young bucks today who are on a quest, I figure."

"Sioux?"

"Yes, they looked like it from the distance."

"They were probably the ones shot those arrows I found in that grizzly. That was why the big one was so mad. They'd wounded him." She shook her head in disgust.

"So now you have to be grateful to the Sioux." He chuckled at his joke.

"Never," she said, looking mad about it, and carried off the armload of saddle to the cabin.

His side improved over the next few days and he sawed some firewood, concerned about the small supply on hand. In the cabin, hidden in the back of the box cupboard, he found a letter addressed to Robespierre Le Blanc, General Delivery, Cross Creek, Wyoming Territory. It was two years old by the date and was from his wife, written in very flowery handwriting. The farm was doing well and she expected to sell thirty fat pigs that fall for seventy dollars apiece if the market held. She would expect to see him the following spring or summer when he came in with his furs.

Slocum wondered if that was the mystery man who'd kidnapped Easter. If so, Le Blanc must not have gone home after he sold the furs. No telling. Maybe later Slocum would go into Cross Creek and see if they knew anything about him.

"He didn't have any money?" he asked her when he finished reading it.

"I didn't look. His things are over there," she said with a

toss of her head. Slocum took the cup of coffee she offered him and patted a spot on the bed for her to sit.

He blew on the steam and looked at her. "I'm getting much better."

Her eyebrows raised and she jumped up, about spilling his coffee.

"Good." Her fingers tore at the strings holding her skirt. Wild-eyed, she looked hard at him for his response.

He rose and nodded in approval as he toed off his boots. In his stocking feet, he crossed the hand-hewed flooring and barred the door with the large wooden plank.

"No interruptions," he said, and walked back.

She was standing naked, huddled, with her arms folded over her teardrop breasts in the dim glow let in by the glass bottles lined in frames that made the two windows. A shadowy light spread over her tawny body, and the sight of her sensuous beauty took his breath away as he hurried to undress. In seconds, the room's cool air swept his bare skin. He reached out and clutched her against his chest, his lips seeking hers.

At first, her mouth was unmoved under his; then her brown eyes flew open and she threw her arms around his neck. His tongue sought hers, and quickly their mouths became welded to each other. In a quick sweep, he picked her up and carried her to the bed. Lost in the intoxication of making love, kissing, tasting, nibbling, they soon snuggled in the arms of desire under the quilts, building a warmth that drove the room's chill from their skin. Her slight awkwardness at the start soon dissolved into a fiery passion and she forced herself toward him—against him, with her obvious need rising like a boiler thermometer under full steam.

She spread her legs apart and he slipped between them. He nosed the head of his erection in the moist gates. And her heavy breathing was the only sound in the cabin as he regained his own. Restraining the force in his butt that desired to be inside her, he began to gently probe her. When he reached her ring of fire, the resistance was powerful, and he braced himself over her to put more effort with each stroke.

Then he gave a harder push, and it parted with a small cry from her as she clutched him. At last, he was working in her confines, savoring every moment of the first ride. Under him, she grinned in pleasure, tossed her head on the mattress, and clung to his arms. She raised her butt up to receive all of him, and soon their public bones were rubbing together.

Then he knew from the rising force that he was about to come, and in a wild surge to give her as much as he could, he pounded her faster and harder. In a wild flurry, he came and they both collapsed.

They spent the rest of the day cuddled in each other's arms and making love. It became a soft honeymoon between two lovers on a rope bed that was the only thing to protest the breaks from their reverie.

It was close to dark when she scrambled from under the covers, quickly dressed, and began to fix them some food to eat. The look of regret written on her face over having to leave their nest was not wasted on him. He rose, dressed, went over to where she worked to make biscuit dough in a metal pan, and gave her a deep kiss.

"I'm going to check on the horses," he said, pulling on his boots with a twinge of pain in his side. Funny, he'd never noticed it making love to her. Oh, well—

Winchester in his hands, and dressed in his jumper, he stepped outside to study the underbelly of a gray sky. Snow wasn't far away. He first climbed up to the small lake and surveyed the upper end of the valley. Nothing looked out of place up there. A mule deer buck crossed the meadow at too great a distance for his gun. What did she say she wanted? A moose. A woman always wanted something hard, though a good fat moose would make great eating for a couple of months for the two of them. They might need to make a hunting trip before winter had them in its icy grasp and find themselves a good one.

He found the horses and mules in the lower end of the valley. They looked up and considered him, then went back to grazing as the shadows lengthened and the sun set the ridge beyond on fire behind the cloud cover. Satisfied and listening to a scolding pair of ravens flying over his head, he started back for the cabin's warmth. He'd been in much worse deals than this one.

Snow began to sift out and the first wet flakes fell on his face. It covered the ground by the time he reached the cabin. He burst in and showed her the white flakes swirling around on wind gusts.

"Winter is here?"

"No." He shook his head. "It's only a warning." He hugged her from behind and rocked her in his arms. "It will warm up one more time or two, then shut in. We can make a trip to Cross Creek to get some supplies. Then I'll move the horses and mules lower down to a valley where they can find feed."

"Will someone steal them?"

"No, I think they'll be fine. They may stray, but we'll get them up next spring."

"Then what?"

"There are other men that look for me. They may come any time and I would have to leave you."

"This Red Dog?"

"No, these're lawmen and they too hound my back trail."

She nodded, looking at him. "Then we better have lots of fun until you have to go." Her laughter rang as she went for the coffeepot. "We have plenty busy winter, huh?"

"Plenty busy."

He smiled, looking at her. No one he could ask for would be a better person to spend the coming season with. As she stood before him pouring the hot coffee into his tin cup, they shared a private look of anticipation. The winter would fly by fast for him in her company.

They were getting ready for bed. She was taking a sponge bath when someone began hollering outside. "Henry Davis, you ole squaw fucker, get up. Me and Cutter's here. Gaw-damnit, get up and put some food on. Why, we're hungrier than a bear coming out of hibernation. Get your ass up."

Slocum waited for her to dress, then, gun in hand, went to the door and slid the bolt over, using his shoulder to hold the door in case they charged it.

"Henry Davis ain't here," he said.

"Well, gol-durn, where is he?"

In the shaft of light from the partially open door, Slocum could see a man in a Texas hat and sheepherder's jacket coated in wet snow standing out there and looking in disbelief at him.

"Ain't no Henry here. The man who previously owned it was killed by a grizzly a week or so ago."

"Cutter, be prepared for some real bad news," the first one said to his pard, who was joining him.

A taller drink of water, he wore a blanket for a coat and a wool scarf around his neck. Batting his eyes, he moved beside his companion. "What the hell happened to our old pard?"

"A grizzly got him. 'Bout a week ago?" the first man asked Slocum.

"Yes. Come in, but watch your language. The lady here was raised in a mission."

Both swept their hats off and nodded to him.

"No cussing, Cutter, she's churchy."

"Like my maw. No gawdamn cussing allowed in her house. No, sirree. She'd whack your ass and feed yeah lye soap."

"Damnit, act like you're home then."

"I will. I will."

"He's Cutter Tennet and I'm Roland Reilly. We knowed ole Davis for twenty years. We been by here to see him couple of times. Figured we could get in out of the snow." Roland looked hard at Easter and blinked in the candlelight. "Why, she sure ain't the same woman was here last summer."

"She's new too. Her name is Easter, mine's Slocum. There's a fairly fresh grave up on the hill with some Sioux trinkets on it."

"Yes, sir, his last one was a Sioux all right. Blue Bell was what he called the last one," Roland agreed after checking with his partner, who nodded in approval.

"Antelope was a better one than that old crabby Sioux," Cutter said, speaking to no one in particular and shaking his head in disapproval.

Easter began rattling pans, firing up the sheet-iron stove like she'd expected them. The two removed their outerwear and piled it by the door.

"Tell me about Henry Davis," Slocum said when they took seats at the table.

"Henry shot a man. Had to leave Texas. He come up here with a cattle herd and took up trapping and looking for gold. Said he had a good claim in Montana, but got into a scrape up there and had to leave it. I seen some of the free gold."

"He had little of anything on him."

"Must of spent it. How did he get into it with a bear?" Roland asked.

"She said it was wounded with arrows and it must have been laying up there in the mud around the lake. Anyone came around, it got mad and charged 'em."

"Where's that bugger at now?"

"Skinned. I shot it the next day. She said Davis was going after water and wasn't armed."

"Mighty handy, you coming along and finding his woman and this place open." Roland frowned in suspicion at him.

Suppressing his anger, Slocum scowled at him. "Now just what do you mean?"

"Henry Davis was a veteran. Shot his share of bluebel-lies."

"Well, I did too. Who's Robespierre?"

"Him and Henry was partners. He went out one time to run his traplines and never come in."

"Could he read?"

Roland shook his head. "I don't reckon so. Henry never learned either. Why?"

"Robespierrre had a wife back East he left behind to run a farm."

"Old Frenchy said she nagged at him all the time," Cutter said as if to dismiss her. "Why, Frenchy had him a squaw of his own that fall we was up here and met him. I can't recall her name, but she sure had a big ass as I re—" He slapped a hand over his mouth. "I never meant to say that."

"It's fine. Wonder what killed him," Slocum said.

"Henry never knew," Roland put in with a grim face. "Said that he didn't find his remains till the next spring. These old mountains can sure be the devil in winter, I guess."

Slocum nodded. He watched Easter serve some leftover bear tracks on a wooden slab to the excited pair.

"Whew-ee," Cutter said with excitement dancing in his blue eyes. "You've done got you a real good'un. Been years since I had bear tracks. Girl, you are sure 'nough a real blessing."

The men slurped up the stew she heated and served them. Then Slocum told them they could sleep on the floor inside, and they all turned in. They thanked her for the food and hospitality. Their bedrolls strung out, they were soon under the covers.

She undressed under the covers. "Will they be here long?" she whispered in his ear while snuggled close to him.

He shook his head.

"Good," she said, and patted his muscle-corded belly as her hard breasts stuck in his back.

He hoped he was right about his assessment of their departure. His half-hard dick told him if they had stayed away, he'd have been using his rising sword on her again. *Damn.*

4

Huddled under a blanket in the cave, Red Dog was cold and pissed off. His empty stomach growled at him. They didn't dare start a fire and risk drawing the posse to them. All their supplies and saddles had been lost in the frantic escape. Along with half of their horses—horses he'd intended to sell for cash money.

Who had sicced the posse after them? Maybe the tall one who stole their money, who called himself Tom White. Red Dog never did trust that bastard, and when White took the whip away from him while he was beating his own dumb squaw who needed it—he'd gotten red-eyed mad. But instead of kicking him half to death and thinking they'd done him in, Red Dog should have sliced his throat. Never again would he leave someone for dead and not cut his throat. But how they would survive with the snow piling up outside, he had no idea. They'd lost their coats and all the blankets but the one she took with her and that now rested on his shoulders.

Snake had taken one of the posse's saddled horses with a bedroll. He shared those quilts with Tar Boy. Everyone had some of the dry cheese and stale crackers they'd found in the posseman's saddlebags the day before. Snake and Tar Boy were out scouting their rabbit snares. Maybe they'd bring in something to eat. They might have to eat them raw, but at least the bear that used this den wasn't around. The place stunk of bear shit and piss—it had been hard to get the horses inside it too.

Mia pointed at the opening. "Someone comes."

Red Dog sat up and cocked his pistol. At the sight of a familiar hat, he undid the hammer and spun it back to the empty chamber. "What you get?"

"Three sage hens and two rabbits." Tar Boy held up the rabbits like prizes.

"How did you get the hens?"

"With sticks," Tar Boy said.

"Where's Snake?" He brushed off the seat of his pants while standing up.

"He be doing some scouting."

"Good," Red Dog said to him, watching Mia take the stiff rabbits. "Make a very small fire. No smoke."

She nodded and carried them to a large rock closer to the opening, where she began to skin them.

"Can we water the horses?" Red Dog asked.

"I never seed no water the whole time I was out there."

"They can live a while without feed, but they don't get water they may twist a gut. You see any willows?"

"Some. Why?"

"After we eat, she can go get some to feed them."

"How we's going to water 'em?"

"We ain't got a kettle to melt any in—" Red Dog shook his head over the impossibility of such a task. How did they get in such messes? Must be some witch had cast a spell on him. That dumb Mia hadn't—she wasn't smart enough. White men like Tom White couldn't put curses on someone unless they were witch doctors. White was no medicine man.

Snake came in an hour later when the blackened rabbits were ready to eat. He slung down four sage hens. Tar Boy gave him half of his rabbit. Red Dog kept all of his and told Mia to fix the sage hens. She never showed any emotion, but set in pulling handfuls of gray feathers from the first one. In her world, the man ate first, then what bones were left the woman and children sucked on.

"You see anything out there?" Red Dog asked.

"Some Sioux in the mountains," Snake said with his mouth full.

"Sioux? What the fuck're they doing here?"

Snake shook his head. "I see some tracks. Maybe three. Maybe more."

"Where do they have a camp?"

Snake finished sucking on a white bone and he discarded it. "I go see. Maybe they have rifles and saddles we can take from them."

Red Dog nodded. "Horses need water, but their tracks would lead them to the cave."

"I go find Sioux camp."

"Good, we'll wait here."

Mia brought the dark bird livers to Snake, holding them out on her hand for him to take.

He nodded in approval and tugged on Tar Boy's sleeve. "Get sage hen power," he said.

Tar Boy took one and popped it in his mouth. Chewing on it, he grinned at them. Red Dog didn't want any and told the others to eat it. He'd eat raw elk or buffalo liver, but bird liver was not for him.

Snake left them before the hens were cooked and slipped away as was his practice. Tar Boy took a nap rolled up in one of the quilts. Red Dog sent Mia to get Snake's quilt and told her to make a pallet for them. When she finished, she undressed and went under the covers. He left his place on the rock and crawled in with her. He pushed her raised knees wide apart and with his pants open, he jerked on his dick as he lowered himself on top of her.

He stabbed the nose of his hard-on into her cunt, then braced himself above her and slammed it deep inside her. When she cried out, he smiled down at her. She was getting what she deserved. He began to pump his prick into her harder and harder. He knew when he plowed this deep into her, she'd soon grow excited and her breathing would speed up. Then the walls of her pussy would begin to contract around his swollen rod. His left nut ached, it had been almost two days since he'd had any.

Furiously, he attacked her until at last he felt an unseen iron hand squeeze both his balls. He jammed his strained dick into her and blew the head off it in a long agonizing stream that made his asshole cramp in pain. Finally growing faint, he stiffened his arms braced over her.

He needed a fresh one. This one wasn't pretty and her breasts had no meat in them. First chance he got, he'd send her away. But not before he found a fresh one. He put his hand on top of her head and pushed her down so she slid underneath him until she could take his dick in her mouth. Then he began pumping it to her. While she sucked hard on it, she used one hand to jerk off the shaft and the other to cuddle his balls. In minutes he had another orgasm, and he felt the tender head of his tool against the roof of her small mouth spewing plenty into it.

Good, she was swallowing it. He smiled. A new woman— he'd wearied of this one.

Snake returned after sundown. He'd found a discarded lard bucket to melt snow in and water the horses.

"What about the Sioux?" Dog asked

"They are only boys on a quest."

"Can we sneak up and kill them?"

Snake shook his head. "They have a few ponies. No rifles. They aren't worth the trouble."

Dog hugged his arms against the cold. He'd wearied of the cave. "We need supplies and a warm place."

"We need to sneak out and find a settler to rob and use his place."

Red Dog nodded, but that would leave tracks for the posse. "How far away is the posse?"

Snake shrugged. "Two, three days."

"In this damn snow any dumb bastard can track you."

"Several new settlers on rivers."

"Lower down." Red Dog shook his head in disgust at the notion. They needed to do something. Their horses would soon be too weak to get through the snow. He agreed with a nod. "We better go find some or starve."

"What we's doing?" Tar Boy asked, joining them.

"We going downhill and find us some settlers to resupply us."

He nodded. "We's sure do need to do that."

"Come sunup, we be going." Red Dog shook his head at his own words. That damn black would have him talking like him pretty soon.

The next morning, a Chinook wind had swept in during the night and the world of white soon became runny slop. They rode till mid-morning, and then let their ponies graze on some exposed grass in the open country. Red Dog felt better about the thaw. Snake stayed on the prowl looking for any sign of a posse. They'd crossed lots of country by late afternoon, and even shot a fat deer. The feast that evening was one of gluttony—they ate over half the carcass celebrating the day's successes.

Red Dog was too full when he fell in the blankets to even consider Mia's ass. He awoke under a sky of bright stars and went off to squat and break wind. Half-nauseated at his overindulgence in eating, he felt the cool wind sweep his bare butt as he strained hard for some relief. They had much to find—saddles, arms, and supplies. Who led that posse? The badge in Dog's pocket might tell him more if he could read.

More grunting from Red Dog, and the only answer was a loud fart and he swore some more. His belly really hurt. They'd have much raiding to do to ever get his bunch reequipped. "Ah," escaped his lips, but it was only more wind he lost.

They rode out at dawn like hungover dogs after a gut feast. They'd be out of the mountains in another day and down on the rolling prairie that footed the front range. A saddle couldn't come too soon—his horse's backbone was making his asshole sore from riding bareback.

The weather warmed and, out scouting, Snake discovered a camp in the foothills. He rode back and told Dog all about two hunters and their outfit.

"Three horses, two mules, a nice army tent—" The breed squatted by the small fire where Red Dog sat on the blanket and Mia cooked the sage hens Dog had shot earlier.

"They army?"

"No, Texas—I hear 'em talk."

"Might be drovers, huh?" Dog was already counting the money they might have on them from some cattle sale.

Snake nodded. "They be easy to take."

With a shake of his head, Dog scowled. "They might be tough. They're liable to be well armed and be handy with the weapons."

"Good horses, good tent, pack mules," Snake said, acting as anxious as Dog had ever seen him.

Food too. They better make plans on taking them. "How far away are they?"

"Maybe hour ride."

"We can't ride into that canyon. The horses' sounds coming down would wake them."

Snake gave a toss of his head. "She can hold the horses."

"All right, we go down there and take them tonight. Make it look like them Sioux did it." Dog laughed out loud and slapped Snake on the shoulder. "Good job."

After dark, they mounted up and pushed off the mountain. They wound their way under the stars off the steep sides until the sounds of a small stream joined their descent. The dim trail wound around and crossed the water several times. Snake held up his hand and vaulted off his horse.

The rear guard, Tar Boy, rode in and dismounted. Mia was busy gathering the leads and reins. Dog told them to be very quiet, and then he threw his leg over and slipped off his horse. On his feet, he pulled the pants out of his crotch and winced at his sore rectum. Their plan better go well.

They left Mia and hurried through the dark timber. A wolf high above them on the rim cut loose, and his cry echoed. Dog wanted to shut him up—might wake the hunters. Without a pause for concern, Snake moved on. They eased by the snoring horses and mules on a picket line. The strong ammonia stink of their urine scalded Dog's nose, but they looked like fine, stout animals in the darkness.

Snake halted at the edge of the camp. On his haunches, Dog squatted. The smoke from the dying fire burned his eyes and nostrils as he surveyed the dark camp. Nothing stirred.

Then, above the small creek's rush, he heard the sounds of someone snoring. Dog nodded his approval. Even in the starlight, he could see that the camp setup indicated wealth.

He gave a nod for Snake to lead the way. Each man had out his own large sharp knife. They hesitated at the edge of the tent. Snake tried the flap and it was not tied. They exchanged nods. Dog changed hands with his knife, wiped his wet palm, and then regripped the elkhorn handle.

"Go," he said in a soft whisper.

Snake went in first and went left. On his heels, Dog stepped right, and he could hear the man snoring on his side of the tent. Knife poised to strike, he half-stumbled in the darkness over a saddle on the ground. Recovering, he drove the blade deep into the blanketed form.

A strangled scream came from the left. "They got me—"

Dog ignored the man's words, repeatedly stabbing the struggling form on the right until his hand at last grasped the victim's hair and he slashed his throat in a final swipe.

Satisfied the man was dead, he sat on the ground, out of breath and trembling all over. Finally, he shouted for Tar Boy to bring a light. Wiping the blade off on his pants, he realized from the wetness in his crotch that he'd ejaculated.

"Sumbitch die hard," Snake grumbled when Tar Boy lifted the flap and held up the coal oil light to illuminate the bloody massacre.

"Drag 'em outside and scalp 'em," Dog ordered as he struggled to stand. They needed to make it appear like the Sioux had been responsible. The copper smell of blood and the sourness of severed guts made the atmosphere in the tent hard to take. He felt better outside in the starlight.

When Snake and Tar Boy pulled the first body outside, Dog dropped on his knees and began to search it for money. "Hold the light," he shouted at Mia.

It was the money belt he felt first. A canvas belt bulged under the corpse's shirt. He ripped the shirt open in the dim light and then undid the buckles and jerked the belt free. Hefting the weight of it, he smiled to himself—lots of real money in it. They'd found a treasure.

The twosome brought out the second body and dumped it on the ground. "What you find?" Snake asked.

"Maybe our ticket out of here."

"Huh?"

Dog shook his head in disgust at the breed's stupidity. "I mean the money to go where we want to go."

Snake made a face. "I don't want to go anywhere else."

"Good, then you stay here." No use even talking to him. He was a blanket-ass Injun and beyond saving. Dog checked the first pouch on the belt. Full of shiny twenty-dollar gold pieces that spilled out and amazed Dog. Those two must have sold a large herd or something.

"Maybe buy us women," Snake said to Dog, motioning toward Tar Boy.

"Maybe," Dog said. "Get their clothing off them. It must look like those Sioux did this."

"Why? Who cares who killed them?" Snake asked.

"'Cause the law will find them and look for their killers."

"Hmm, looks like lots of work for nothing," Snake grumbled.

"Come on, Snake, we can do it," Tar Boy said, stepping in before Dog expressed his growing wrath at the breed.

"Good. Make us some food," Dog said to Mia. "Cut the loin off that deer they have hanging."

She ran off to obey him as he put the coins away in the pouches. They possessed a good tent, saddles, supplies, horses, and money—lots of money. These Texans had been an easy kill. Maybe he would go to town and find some whiskey and a white whore. It might change his luck—besides, he needed a better-looking woman than Mia.

He smiled to himself over his plans as he watched Tar Boy and Snake strip the two bodies of their clothing. There was lots to do. But he was smart enough to do it. The finger must point at the Sioux when the law found the mutilated bodies, and the trail must lead the whites to the Sioux camp.

5

Slocum decided that with the two cowboys to watch things and protect Easter, he'd make a fast trip to Cross Creek and buy some supplies they'd need for the winter. She listed flour, baking powder, dried beans, oats, raisins, sugar, salt, and some matches as the main items. He wanted ammunition for his pistol and rifle too.

Cutter and Roland agreed to stay over. So he and Easter went after the mules to use as his pack animals. They rode Paint double and found the pair down the far end of the meadow.

"You will come back?" she asked, pausing before slipping off from behind him.

"Yes."

"Good," she said, and slid off Paint's rump. With a rope in hand, she went after the mules ten yards away. They acted suspicious for a moment at the figure in her swirling fringe approaching them. But after a snort or two, her seductive words settled them and she fashioned a halter on one and led it back to Slocum.

He took the lead rope and motioned to the second one.

"The other one won't be left out." She laughed, and was soon behind him on the saddle, hugging him tight. The mules came after them.

41

"You never had a white wife?" she asked.

"No."

Her cheek resting on his back, she made a scolding sound. "Ah, such a shame. I can only think what she missed."

"Why do you worry about a white woman you don't know?" he asked as the cabin came into sight.

"I only worry because it has been three days since we did it. See how long I have waited for you!"

He reached back and patted her leg. "I get the message. It's warm enough that the men can sleep outside tonight."

"Good." She hugged him tighter.

That night, with the cabin to themselves, they made love until at last they collapsed in each other's arms and slept until dawn. Before the sun cracked dawn, they awoke and she hurried about to fix their breakfast in the lamplight.

"You will be careful in that place."

Seated at the table, sipping his coffee, he nodded. "Careful as I can be."

"Good. Don't be gone for too long." With a wink, she went and unbarred the door to let the men in.

"Morning," Cutter said. "Roland's gone after a fat deer we saw sneaking up to the lake."

"We can use the fresh meat," she said, busy putting the golden biscuits and bowl of gravy on the table.

"He's going to miss breakfast is all," Cutter said, and laughed.

"I'll cook him some more," she said. "If he brings in a deer."

"I'd hate for Roland to starve," Slocum said. "Guess he better kill it."

They laughed and the two men settled in at the table, busy eating and talking about the mild weather. She went outside and returned.

"He got it. He's bringing it in right now."

"I thought I heard a shot," Cutter said between forks full of gravy-dripping biscuits.

Slocum nodded in agreement. "I heard one."

Roland arrived, and they went out to see his large buck in

the gray light. The deer was strung up to be skinned and gutted. Then they went back inside.

"Twelve points," Roland said to her. "Fat as a town dog."

"Good," Easter said, getting out more biscuits from the Dutch oven. "Better eat or they'll have it all gone."

"Well, I figured we needed it." Roland looked around.

"Sure did and thank you," Slocum said, slipping on his coat. "I'll see the three of you in a couple of days. I'm off to Cross Creek for supplies, and I won't forget a little cheer and some tobacco."

He gave Easter a hug and went out to saddle his animals. In minutes, she joined him and helped him. When everything was ready, he swept her up, hugged and kissed her. "I'll be back."

Then Slocum swung in the saddle and headed out. She reached out to clap him on the leg and smiled as he rode away. "See you soon," he said.

He cut for the south end of the big meadow. A few elk flushed at his approach and headed for the timber. He ignored them and rode on. When he struck the wagon ruts about mid-morning, he made the animals trot. The road followed a small creek, and he watched for a moose in the willows. But none was in sight. By evening, he was at the eastern brink of the Big Horns, and dropped off into a dark canyon that contained a loud creek. Even the starlight hardly penetrated the pine boughs overhead, but Paint was a good night horse, so Slocum put his trust in him and rode on.

On the flats after the moon rose, he made a dry camp and put nose bags of corn on the animals, leaving them tied. At dawn, he rubbed his gritty eyes and relieved his bladder, then cinched up and rode for Cross Creek. He had not intented to ride into the village without scouting it some. In his cautiousness, he circled and came in at the rear of the wagon yard.

He dismounted behind the raw lumber structure and hitched his animals to the corral. The mules were honking, but he ignored them. A swamper came out rubbing his whisker-bristled mouth with his palm.

"Howdy."

"Any strangers in town?"

"Not that I seen. Who're you looking for?"

"Couple of breeds and a black I ran into up north."

The swamper cleared his mouth again and shook his uncombed mop. "Ain't seen 'em."

"Good. Them animals be all right there while I get supplies?" He pressed a silver dollar cartwheel in the man's calloused hand.

A grin parted his tobacco-stained lips and exposed his rotten teeth. "They're fine there till hell freezes over, mister."

"Anything suspicious shows up, send me word."

"Couple of hunters're missing." The old man indicated the Big Horns. "The one fella's wife's offering a reward."

"How much?"

"A hundred. They were supposed to be back yesterday. I figured they just found some big bull elk and are trying to get him packed out."

"Never saw them."

"Guess she'll be getting up a party to go find them."

"Thanks, I could use the reward."

The man nodded. "I'm Marty. You need anything, just ask me."

"Tom White's mine," Slocum said with a nod and went through the shadowy, cobwebbed barn, half full with horses standing in tie stalls. The winey-smelling horse piss was strong in his nose. He paused a few feet back from the doorway and studied the street, empty save for a wagon and team across the street in front of Gravette's Mercantile. Out of habit, he shifted the gun on his waist and pulled down his hat brim before he started across the dry rutted street. He reached the store's porch and in the shadows paused to look over the rest of the one-block business district. Nothing looked out of place. Some lunger was coughing his guts up, dumping a mop pail off in the dirt down in front of the Magpie Saloon.

A tall, handsome woman was strolling down the opposite boardwalk with a parasol on her shoulder. Kind of fancy-dressed for a place like Cross Creek. No dove, she carried herself like she belonged to respectable society.

He turned and went inside the store illuminated by coal oil lamps. A clerk looked up like some private in a barracks when an officer had entered.

"Yes, sir," the fresh-faced boy in the white apron said. "May I help you?"

"I need some supplies."

"Will this be cash or charge, sir?"

"Cash."

"Very good. I am not the one approves credit is why I asked. I'm Jim."

"No problem, Jim." And Slocum began to list the items he wanted: beans, flour, baking powder, coffee, etcetera.

The youth moved swiftly to fill his needs. While Slocum stood at the counter, the small silver bells over the door rang and he turned to see the lovely lady sweep inside.

"That's Mrs. McCullem," Jim said in a low voice. "Her husband is missing."

Slocum nodded. "Marty at the stables mentioned it to me when I arrived. Said they were only a day overdue."

Jim made a face and shook his head. "More like four now."

"They'll probably ride in any day." Slocum took off his hat for the woman.

"Do you live here, sir?" she asked, looking him over.

"No, ma'am. Why do you ask?"

"I'm looking to hire some men to go into the mountains and search for my husband."

"What about the sheriff?"

"He doesn't think there is anything wrong with my husband being overdue on his return."

Slocum nodded. "I suppose we could look for him."

"You and who else?"

"Some Texas cowboys staying at my cabin up there." He motioned toward the direction of the mountains.

"My husband is from Texas. Perhaps they know him."

"I can ask them."

"His name is Josh McCullem. He owns the M Bar Ranch."

The name was familiar to Slocum, though he'd never met

the man. He merely acknowledged he'd heard her. Somewhere in the recesses of his mind, he knew or had heard something about her man—good or bad, it remained beyond his recall.

"I'm sorry—" She broke into his deep reflection. "My name is Lilly McCullem."

"Tom White," he said and nodded, replacing his hat. "I'm sure that my friends would agree to searching for him."

"Then may I hire you?"

"I'm not sure what to say. We'll look for him and let you know what we find."

"Mr. White—" She straightened her shoulders so her proud breasts pushed out the dress. "I am a proficient horseback rider and have been on two long cattle drives. I need no special attention. I am ready to pay for your services as guide. When may we leave?"

With a mild smile for her, he nodded. "As soon as I get these supplies on my mules."

The bell rang and a burly-looking man with whiskers and dressed in overalls stalked into the store.

"Ah, thar you are," he said, and headed for Mrs. McCullem.

Her blue eyes looked troubled. Then her dark lids narrowed and her mouth set in a tight line. "Mr. Yarnell, I have told you I have no need of your services."

"Aw, lady—" He rolled his cud of tobacco around in his mouth looking at her like he would a raw piece of beef. "I'm ready to go find your man."

She shook her head. "Mr. White is going to handle that for me."

"Huh?" He blinked his bleary eyes in disbelief at her, then craned his head around to look at Slocum.

"Why, that sumbitch couldn't find his ass with both hands—" His words were cut short by the barrel of Slocum's .44 punching him in the stomach.

"Apologize to her," Slocum said in a cutting tone as he drove the man backward toward the door. The eyes of customers and clerks flew open in frozen shock as they watched him make the big man retreat rapidly toward the entrance at the point of his six-gun. He opened the left-side door with his left hand and drove the intruder out on the boardwalk.

"Now get lost."

"You ain't seen the last of me, White. I'll nail your gaw-damned hide to my shithouse door." He waved a dirty index finger at Slocum as he almost toppled off the edge of the walk. Catching his balance, he spit out a mouthful of to-bacco and wiped his lips on the back of a big ham of a hand.

"Just don't cuss in front of a lady again unless you have on your Sunday suit."

The big man frowned at him. "Huh?"

"'Cause they'll bury you in them overalls. Now get the hell out of here."

"You ain't heard the last of Rube Yarnell, White. No, sir." He waved a threatening finger at Slocum like a gun as he backed across the street.

Slocum holstered his gun and went back inside. Mrs. Mc-Cullem stood a few feet from the door. "I am so sorry. The man has been insisting I hire him."

As the door closed, Slocum turned to her to allay her con-cern. "How far away is your horse?"

"I can be ready in fifteen minutes."

"I'll be at the livery."

She looked around as if to make certain she wouldn't be heard, then spoke softly. "I'm not a bad judge of men. I con-sidered you a man of action. Thank you."

Slocum opened the door for her and she swept past him with a rustle of her dress. So much for a quiet winter with Easter—somehow he had a notion his life was going to be turned upside down by this woman and her situation.

6

Dog wore the heavy money belt around his waist under his leather shirt. He couldn't stop from touching the solid shape of it. More money than he'd ever possessed in his life. More money than he took in that stage holdup in Nebraska. More than when he cleaned out the steel safe at the trader's outpost on the Platte. Enough money to buy a place—but where?

He booted his thin horse down the slope. There had to be a place where he wasn't an outlaw and could live out his life. But he couldn't read and barely could count—business people could do such things. They'd rob him like the store man did his mother. When he was a boy, she took three prime wolf skins to this man's store. He gave her some candy, some wormy flour, and told her she owed him a dollar.

From under his hat brim, he checked the sun time. Past noon already. He wouldn't be to Cross Creek before late afternoon. No matter. With all his money, he could buy what he needed and impress the white people. Even a breed who had money could be a big man. His mouth filled with saliva. Whiskey—plenty of whiskey—he could buy plenty of it. No cheap rotgut firewater, but the real smooth kind that went down a man's throat like velvet.

He glanced back as Mia dragged the mules on their leads. Even without packs, they led stubbornly. Impatient with them and her, he turned his horse out and rode past her, flailing her with the quirt on his right wrist as he did so. She ducked over in the saddle and his lash fell on her leather shirt.

"Keep them moving!" He spurred his horse behind them, reached out, and quirted both mules on the their butts, spooking them so much they about overwhelmed Mia in their panic. She rode off in a high lope.

Standing in the stirrups, he realized he had to keep the mules out of sight at Cross Creek. That was why he hadn't ridden one of the Texans' good horses to town. No problem. Mia could stay with the mules at the outskirts. After dark, he'd load them and they'd be gone. The notion of being linked to the murders raised gooseflesh on the back of his arms despite the midday sun's heat that even melted the snow under bushes.

He felt the thick wad bound around his waist and smiled. If that lazy bitch didn't keep up from here on to town, he'd beat her good too. With his horse in a trot, he left the timber and started across the wide-open meadow. Nothing was in sight in the vast basin. He stood in the stirrups of the good saddle with M Bar stamped on the fenders, but he'd used part of a plaid blanket over it to hide the marks. Most Injuns did that anyway, covered their saddle with blankets. Where could he go to live out his life as a king?

Would the Sioux accept him at the Wounded Knee Reservation? He was their kin. No matter the full-bloods scowled at breeds. Maybe a rich one might be acceptable. Maybe?

They reached Cross Creek near sundown. He made Mia stay out of sight in the canyon by the small stream and went into the town. Before he'd left her, he'd promised her candy if all went well. Numbly, she'd nodded. He smiled to himself, riding down the narrow trail. At last she'd bowed her head to him. He would soon have her broken to his will. No more of that open laughing and show-off riding like she was some kind of a princess instead of his slave. She was learning her place. But with his money, he could buy a woman with pointed tits and a tighter pussy. Maybe he'd do that.

He tied his horse in back of the stables in the pines and

checked his Colt in the half-light. Then he eased his way downhill and took a place at the side of the livery. A few horses were hitched at the racks. Several freight wagons were parked in the streets, and some men off-loaded one in front of the big store. Carrying hundred-pound sacks on their shoulders, they went into the lighted doorway.

He squatted in the growing darkness and rubbed his hands on his pants. Time to move. He strode across the street and fell in behind a clerk carrying a sack. Inside that store, which smelled of spices, leathers, and coal oil, he went to the counter in the rear.

The old man who owned the store wiped his hands on his apron and nodded to him from behind the counter. "What do you need?"

"Sack of flour, sack of dry beans, four slabs bacon—"

The man held out his hand. "That's way over twenty dollars."

Dog raised his chest and nodded—then in his best Injun voice said, "Me got money."

"Fine, so you understand," the owner said, and bent over with his pencil to write down the rest on the butcher paper.

"Coffee, baking powder . . ." Dog went on with his list, making the man look up and frown.

Angry at his suspicion, Dog slapped five twenty-dollar gold pieces on the counter.

"That's fine," the man said.

Dog nodded and went on listing things he needed, but a wave of revulsion went through him. He recalled snatching that other storekeeper's hair from behind and slicing his throat when the man stepped out the back door of his store after cheating his mother of her wolf hides. Maybe he would kill this old man the same way.

"You want this tonight?" the owner asked.

Dog nodded. "I go get my mules."

"Very good, sir." He picked up one of the coins and then set it back. "Brand-new."

"Good money," Dog said, as if the man doubted it being real.

"Oh, yes, just don't see much new money."

"Good, I get mules." Dog started to leave.

"Oh, mister, you only owe me twenty-two dollars." He shoved three of the gold pieces back and opened the drawer to make change.

"I knew that," Dog said, and waited for his change. The man must be honest—he for sure knew that Dog couldn't count and could have cheated him. Maybe Dog wouldn't kill him. His fingers closed on the paper money and coins the man gave him back and he nodded.

With money in his pocket, Dog left to get the mules. He caught the horse, then stopped and listened in the growing darkness. Town noises filtered to him. A horse squealed in the livery pens, and the thumping of hind hooves bruising another thudded loudly.

He led his horse up the trail in the darkness. Overhead in the boughs, birds in their roosts fluttered and the stars began to shine. Best he took his goods and left the area. A breed with money might draw suspicion. That store man had been examining those coins with such interest. Dog's senses had kept him alive for this long. He'd better follow them.

"Move a muscle and you're dead, breed," the coarse-sounding voice said.

Dog froze. Was it the law? His hands were quickly thrust tight behind his back in leather thongs and his captors also disarmed him. Rough hands shoved him ahead. Three white men had taken him prisoner. He could smell the cheap whiskey and tobacco on their breath. A big man with a long beard was in charge—the boys called him Rube.

"Build a fire," Rube ordered, and the youngest of the outfit moved to obey.

Where was Mia? The powerful hand on his shoulder shoved him to sit down. Seated, he watched the flare of the matches catch the tinder and illuminate the area around them. He saw Mia with her hands tied. She was seated on a blanket across from him. When he caught her eye, he gave a head shake to tell her not to say anything. The whites knew nothing about the money belt—yet.

"Now how the fuck did you get them mules? They belonged to McCullem?" the big man asked.

Dog never answered.

"You can play that dumb-Injun stuff long as you want. I figure that fancy bitch'll pay me big bucks for you and them mules." Rube folded his arms over his chest. "Yes, sir, and the sheriff'll hang your ass too.

"Get some food going," Rube said to the boys. "You can squeeze these damn Injuns till their guts come out and not learn nothing. We got the goods—mules, and I bet that horse belonged to McCullem too."

The older boy lifted the blanket and shouted, "Hell, it's McCullem's saddle. I seed this brand on it."

"Whatcha say now?" Rube asked Dog, and dropped down beside Mia. He lounged on his side and laughed. "Cat got your tongue?"

Dog never answered.

"Here," Rube said, and freed Mia's wrists. He sat up to lift her leather blouse high enough to expose her small pointed breasts. "Guess I can have me a little Injun pussy while we wait on food, huh, breed?"

No reply. Dog's gaze was concentrated on the fire's flame. His hands behind his back were bound tight, but he intended to work them free. If he ever did, he'd feed that bastard his own dick.

Laughing at his good fortune, Rube got on his knees and removed Mia's blouse over her head. She offered no resistance. Then he settled back on his legs and grinned before he fondled her breasts. At last, he forced her down on the blanket and ran his hand along her skirt.

"My, my, you're going to be a mighty pretty fine piece," he said as he probed her with his finger.

At last, he hurriedly undid the ties at her waist and stripped off the skirt, then tossed it aside. With his mouth open wide issuing streams of drool, he rolled over on his knees and studied her huddled naked figure under him. Not taking his eyes off her, he undid his galluses. He shoved the pants down to his knees so his mushroom ass shone in the firelight. Then with a growl, he roughly parted her legs, climbed on top of her, and poked his erection inside her.

"Not bad pussy," Rube shouted to Dog over his shoulder as he pounded it to her. He laughed as he pumped his dick harder and harder.

The strings grew looser on Dog's wrists, and the slippery blood from where the leather cut into Dog's skin in his desperate effort to get loose helped him slip free at last. But he must not let them know of his success until he could grasp the six-gun in the holster lying only a few feet from the grunting Rube. A rifle leaning against a pine tree a few yards away was too awkward a weapon for him in such close quarters with three of them to kill.

The younger one was frying some bacon, and the middle one, called Jocko, sat to the side, jacking off his dick, getting ready to poke his prod to her when the old man finished. No one watched Dog. Certain of that—Dog moved. He scrambled on his hands and knees for the gun and holster. In a swift jump, he landed and whipped the Colt free of the leather holder and cocked it.

Jocko, with his dick in his hands, screamed like a girl, "Watch out!"

About that time, Rube came and shoved his dick hard up in Mia. "Huh?"

Before Rube could turn and look over his shoulder, the six-gun belched an orange blast in the night and hot lead struck him in the back. He grunted and fell on top of her. Dog rolled to his left side and shot Jocko in the face. In an instant, Dog bounded to his feet and took off after the already fleeing younger one. He didn't want him to escape and go for help.

Pungent sticky evergreen needles swept his arms and face as he ran through the darkness. He could hear the boy moaning as he ran down the canyon through woods, bouncing off stiff boughs and falling down. "No—no—no—don't kill me." His raucous breathing caused a telltale racket. That sound led the fleet-footed Dog to the starlit glen where the boy had collapsed on the ground, holding up his hands and begging for his life.

Dog stopped on the heels of his moccasins, took aim down the blade sight, and shot him. First bullet in the chest and the second at close range in the horrified face.

In the pearl starlight, Dog stood over the thrashing legs of the dying boy. The .45 was like a great sack of rocks in his right hand as he kicked the body when it fell still at last. "Sumbitch."

After all this, he'd sure have to leave the Big Horns. A breed had no right to kill a white man—let alone three of them. No matter that they'd raped his woman and planned to kill him too.

He knew when he shot that bully in Deadwood that he had to flee or be lynched. Now he must run again. Not without the flour, beans, coffee—maybe they hadn't heard the shots in town. He rushed back to camp.

Naked, Mia sat huddled and crying—feeling sorry for herself. He kicked her swiftly in her bare butt. He ignored her complaining. "Get dressed. We must run for the mountains." He found his own gun and holstered it. "Get going!"

"Where?" she cried, tears running down her face.

"To the mountains like all blanket-ass Indians do."

She acted as if she'd lost her mind as he gathered all the horses. At least she finally was dressing.

With all of them in tow, he handed her the reins and gathered all their guns and ammo. He hung the holsters over saddle horns and put the two rifles in scabbards on their horses. Then he went over to where the facedown Rube's bare ass stuck up in the dying firelight, and rolled him on his back.

He jerked his recovered knife from the sheath, bent over, and grasped all of Rube's genitals in one hand and sawed them off. Then he used the blade to pry open Rube's mouth and stuffed them inside. Then he scalped him. Finished, he stepped over to Jocko and did the same to him.

"You won't fuck any more women in the next world," he said to the two dead men, and then bailed on his horse. No time to get those supplies he'd ordered. This place would soon be crawling with white people who'd heard the shooting.

"Bring them," he said to her about the horses and mules. "We must hurry."

Then he booted his horse for the mountains. Damn those three sumbitches anyway.

7

Earlier that day, Slocum and his new employer, Lilly Mc-Cullem, left Cross Creek for the mountains. They went north along the face of the range toward the Elk Creek Trail to check on where she thought her husband might have made his camp.

"Mr. White," she said, pushing her good sorrel horse up beside his. "I really am concerned Josh hasn't returned. It is very unlike him. He's not unreliable."

Slocum looked over at the handsome woman trotting beside him, dressed in men's clothing, including tucking most of her curls under a Boss of the Plains Stetson. Except for her figure, which filled the shirt quite well, she looked more like a boy than the society woman he saw in town. But she was not just a society woman. She could ride.

"I have to tell you something. My name is not White, it's Slocum."

She nodded. "I see."

"Too long for me to explain here, but sometime I will. So call me Slocum."

"Lilly will be fine. I understand that formality in this country is a little out of place." Then she laughed for the first time.

He glanced over at her. "As to your husband—we'll find him."

"I hope so." She chewed on her lower lip, looking straight ahead. "I've prayed a lot that he'll be okay."

"I understand."

At the start of the Elk Creek Trail, he reined them up to let the horses breathe before they started into the canyon. After they cooled, he watered them in the small stream. She went apart from him and with her back to a pine, she looked up at the towering range of granite and pine-clad slopes. Idly, she slapped at her leg with the small quirt on her wrist. He knew she must be in a lot of mental turmoil over the mission ahead.

He led the horses over and motioned toward the yawning seam in the Big Horns. "She's waiting for us."

"Why call it 'she'?" she asked with a smile.

He shrugged his shoulders. "I don't know. Seems more like a woman's job to sit there in one place and hold the rest of the world together."

"I think you're right, Slocum. A woman's job is to hold it all together." She took the reins and started to mount. In one bound, she was in the saddle and nodded to him. "Best we went on."

"Yes, ma'am." He gathered the mules' leads, mounted, and with a nod sent her on ahead.

The trail crossed and recrossed the stream. With her in the lead, they soon left the streambed and took a narrow trail that skirted the tall gray bluff face. Small landslides on the pathway made her sorrel pick his way carefully over them.

"No hurry," Slocum said from behind her, and surveyed the yawning gap behind them. On the opposite slope, a blacktail doe raised her head from grazing and stared across at them. Two weaned fawns nearby also gave them a sharp look, then bolted away stiff-legged into the leafless aspens.

"Trouble ahead," she said, and reined her horse up. He tied the first mule's lead to his saddle horn, knowing Paint would ground-tie. Then, after a glance off to the side into the shadowy depths, he eased down, found enough footing to slip by Paint, and walked up the trail to where the sorrel's butt blocked his way.

She twisted in the saddle to face him. "There's been some falling rock ahead. Is there a wider spot?"

He shook his head. Paint and those mules would stand. If her sorrel got restless and tried to turn, she and the horse would topple off a thousand feet into the canyon. He tried to look past her to see if it was wider ahead. No room.

"Sit tight," he said, spotting a pine snag growing out of the face of the cliff some fifteen feet above her that looked stout enough. He eased back and undid his lariat off the saddle, talking softly to Paint. "I need to get up there and clean enough off to get over it. You sit tight."

He shook out the rope and made a loop. Not wanting to spook the animals, he knew he had to flip it up and over the stubby tree. Whirling the lariat was a luxury he couldn't afford.

Talk to them. "Easy, Paint," he said, and flipped the rope up. No luck. Still talking to the animals in a calm voice, he gathered his lariat and made a new loop and tossed it. This time it went over the tree. Then he went closer to the pine and tried to move the rope farther down toward its base. But his loop closed about halfway down and nothing he did at his end made any difference. He cinched it tight. *Tree hold.*

Hand over hand, he began to climb it, testing the strength. It felt springy under his weight. The sorrel acted snorty with him working so close to his butt.

"I'm going to try it," he said to Lilly. "When I get over you, try to make him back up a few steps and I'll be able to come down ahead of you." *I hope.*

"He's usually good to back up."

"Fine." Just as long as he didn't turn.

Slocum began to climb with his boot soles on the slick rock face as, hand over hand, he pulled himself up the rope. He glanced down at her and decided he needed to be another foot higher to clear the horse. That accomplished, his arms ached and his footing became precarious.

"Back him easy."

He looked down and saw the horse hesitate. *No, don't do that.* Then the sorrel eased some and started to turn to look back. Lilly forced him to look ahead and pulled on the reins, and he resumed his easy shuffle in retreat, his iron shoes scraping on the rock surface.

"Good. Talk to him," Slocum said, anxious to get off the side of the mountain.

Hand over hand, he came down until his boot soles were on solid ground. The sorrel snorted at him, but held his place under her. Out of breath and standing on the ledge at last, Slocum drew deep breaths of air. He nodded his approval at her. Then he turned to the slide.

It was more than ten feet long and he could not see how far around the face of the mountain it went. He began to toss off the large rocks, making a way for their animals. It was slow, tedious work that strained his back and ate up his gloveless hands. He talked to her and assured her she was better in the saddle than off at this point due to the narrowness of the ledge. His work began to show progress, but the sunset was his enemy and it was threatening in the west.

All he wanted was a path. That meant the larger rubble needed to be cleared and a suitable track made over the rest of the slide. He'd worked twelve feet around the bluff face to make a way when he found a mammoth boulder. Without a pole for a pry, he wondered how he'd ever budge it. Damn, the notion of backing the animals down over a mile was impractical.

He put his shoulder to the rock and it teetered a little, to his shock. On his knees, he began to clear all he could reach out from under it. The tips of his fingers bled and in several places, his hands had cuts that turned the rock dust to mud. When he had gotten out all he could, he put his shoulder again to the boulder. It moved, and he strained with his teeth gritted. It began to topple over like a great sawed-off tree, and hung on the edge for an instant, enough to make him afraid it wouldn't go. Then he gave a huge charge forward and caught himself only at the last second when the great rock went roaring down the mountainside into the yawning depths.

He collapsed on his butt, and his lungs had knives in them. With the rock gone, the trail ahead looked all right, and above him he could see the sunset shining in the saddle of the pass.

"Bring him on easy over that stuff. Paint and the mules will come." He scrambled to his feet and brushed his hands off. Leading the way, he glanced back as the sorrel took his time, finding a sound footing with each step before he moved ahead. When Slocum reached the wider trail, he could look downhill and see Paint leading the mules up behind the sorrel. At that point, Slocum's pounding heart let up some.

Where Lilly finally reached the wider trail on the steep mountainside, he went back to stand beside her stirrup. She shook her head as if to dismiss the tension, then stepped down, and her knees threatened to buckle. He caught her in his arms. As if his arms could save her, she crushed herself to him.

"It's fine. We're over the worst," he said.

"Oh, I never thought—" She buried her face in his shoulder.

"It was a tough trip." He held and patted her. "We've made it."

"I have to sit down here," she said. "I am trembling all over."

He agreed. "I'll turn my head."

"Yes," she said, and swallowed.

He went several steps up the mountain and stood with his back to her as she relieved her bladder. Listening to the horses and mules shake off their tensions in a rattle of leather and snorts, he waited until she walked up before he turned back. It had been a close call on the trail.

"You don't think—" She pressed her crooked forefinger to her mouth as if concerned about something. "That-that they went off there?"

"No way to know. We better get up and over this pass. Twilight won't last much longer."

"Certainly."

"I'll help you on your horse."

She looked at him for a second, then agreed. "Thank you.

You do have manners and—and plenty of guts. I couldn't look up at that little tree. I thought it would break."

"Not this time." He boosted her on the sorrel and she straightened in the saddle and gathered her reins.

"I must say this was no trip for the faint of heart."

"No, ma'am." He swung in the saddle and headed Paint for the pass.

Before the last light drained off, he found a flat in some scrubby pines and began to make camp. He built a small fire and made some coffee from his canteen. They used it to wash down the dry cheese and jerky, seated with their bedding on their shoulders against the night wind and dropping temperatures.

"Where would they camp, do you think—" Her words were cut off by the nearby howl of a wolf. She hugged her arms and searched in the night for the animal.

"He's not looking for us. Easier game tonight for him. As for your husband, I have no idea. We'll start searching when we get to the cabin. Cutter and Roland know the area."

'You have a cabin—a ranch up here?"

"I am using a dead man's cabin. He kidnapped an Indian girl and brought her up there. A grizzly killed him when he was going after water."

She laughed aloud, then quickly covered her mouth. "Slocum, you get in all kinds of fixes, don't you?"

"I can find 'em, that's for sure."

"No, I mean, today you saved me, and it sounds like you saved her."

"I've only been doing my part."

"Why do you use an alias?"

"A long time ago a rich man's son got drunk in a card game, picked a fight, and got in the way of a bullet. His father keeps two Kansas deputies on my tail."

"Self-defense?"

Slocum nodded.

"But the law—"

"That belongs to him too. It's been too long ago. I live looking over my shoulder."

"Reckon they followed you today?"

"No, but it's only a matter of time until someone wires them where I am."

She hugged the blankets to her and shuddered. "I see. It will be cold tonight."

"You get too cold, get up and build up the fire."

She looked at the fire. "Perhaps two would be warmer than one. I am not suggesting anything."

"Your call." He waited.

She shrugged. "I believe you are a gentleman. I'll risk it."

"Damn sure be warmer," he said, and spread out his ground cloth.

She excused herself, and a few minutes later came back. They prepared the covers together and when they were ready to crawl under, she smiled at him in the firelight. "You're the second man I ever crawled in bed with."

He nodded and threw some more wood on the crackling fire. Just as long as he wasn't the last. Under the covers, he lay on his side away from her, and she did the same, but shortly she was curled around him and their warmth grew beneath the thick shield of covers.

"You won't ever tell Josh about this, will you?" she whispered.

"Not a word." He hoped for her sake that he had the choice not to tell him. Lost men usually meant one thing—dead men.

Morning came on a soft purple glow. When she stirred, he put his hand on her hip telling her to stay. He crawled out, built up the fire with dry logs, and put on water to boil for coffee.

His coat buttoned, he squatted on the ground, letting the reflective heat wash his face and sore hands against the bitter cold draft that swept the top of the mountain. They had their coffee, and he cinched up the animals, not having unpacked them when he tied them up for the night. They'd find a better place later on, or be at the cabin by dark. There were two places he wanted to check for the missing men. One was a salt lick he knew about that made a great place to camp and watch for game coming in. The other was an old trapper's cabin near Horn Lake.

They rode by that cabin at mid-morning. No sign of anyone camping there. They skirted the small blue lake with Slocum checking for old signs of mule prints since she'd told him the missing men had two pack mules. Mule prints would be different from the usual horse tracks. But there was nothing.

They rode a trail through lots of fallen-down lodgepole pines and reached a large meadow in mid-afternoon. He spotted high in a tree a rag flapping in the wind, and turned Paint in that direction to check on it. What he saw made him whirl the horse and ride back to tell Lilly to stay where she was.

Naked white bodies have a certain look even at a distance. He'd never forgotten the sight of them from the war, on battlefields, in ambushes, unburied.

"You need to stay here," he insisted.

"What-what have you found?" She stood in the stirrups trying to see past him.

He held up his hand to settle her. "There's some dead men over there. I want to go look them over."

Her forefinger pressed to her mouth, she looked close to tears. "Who are they?"

"Who they are I don't know, but it'll be grisly. Trust me."

"What happened?" She was still trying to see past him.

"I'd say it was Indian work."

"Oh, Slocum, I can't stay here."

"Damnit . . ." He dropped his head, shook it in defeat, and turned Paint. He'd done all he could. His stomach curdled and a great stone weighed heavily in it as he approached the remains.

Wild animals had worked on them, he felt certain, and he dismounted fifty feet from them.

"Wait," she said, and dismounted and hurried over to clutch his arm. "Can you see a face?" she asked, looking away and letting him guide her.

"Who had red hair?" he asked.

"Blake did. Oh, no—" He whirled and caught her when her knees buckled and she fainted.

The scene was not pretty. He stood holding her limp weight, gazing at the scalped patches on the men's heads. This was not his first sight of Indian savagery. He'd been a scout with Custer in Kansas, seen plenty of atrocities, but he still wasn't ready for such grisly sights.

Gently, he laid her on the grass and went for blankets. One for her and two to wrap the bodies in. Damn, he hated being forced to be an undertaker. That this might happen had gnawed at him since he'd left Cross Creek with her. Real men never were five days late returning unless they encountered some kind of serious trouble.

She was sitting up when he returned. Her wet eyes were staring into space. "It's him? It's him, isn't it?"

"Lilly, I'm sure it is. When I get them wrapped in blankets, you can look at them. I don't want you to see them till then." He dropped on his knees before her to look in her sad face.

She slung off her hat and looked with pained eyes at him. "Why? Why did they kill them?"

"I can't tell you. Renegades, I guess. They need no reason, their hatred of all whites is so great."

"Who are they?"

"Boys that ran away from the reservation—" He shook his head, unable to alleviate her loss. He reached out and hugged her. "Lilly, I am so sorry I brought you up here. My conscience is eating me up right now. You should have kinfolks—some other woman—I'm not a preacher." He closed his eyes and buried his face in her hair.

A shudder of cold revulsion made him shake all over. Why him? Lord. There was no escaping the senseless loss of good lives in this hard land. She clung to him, and he rocked her back and forth.

They separated and she clutched his forearms. "Slocum, I have to see him."

From around his neck he whipped off his kerchief, and mopped her wet face as easy as he could. "Let me wrap them first." He had no intention of having her look at the savages' madness and the work of wild animals on the bodies.

Sobbing until her shoulders quaked, she took the kerchief, sitting up on her knees, and told him to go ahead.

He wrapped the remains in blankets, roped them tight, and left only their pale faces uncovered. Then he struggled to his feet and not knowing what to say, went back to her.

"You can come tell me if it's them now." He pulled her to her feet.

She clutched his arm. "He must of had thousands of dollars on his body. In a money belt from the herd's sale in Montana. He never trusted banks."

"They took everything." He guided her to the two corpses. Death filled his nose and he remembered the whiskey he'd bought—it might be good. They might both need some.

One look, and she turned back and clutched him. "It's him and Blake. Oh, dear God."

"When you get ready, we'll load them and go to the cabin. I have a pick and a shovel there. They really need to be buried."

"I'm making you do so much for me."

"No, Lilly, don't worry about that."

"But you saved my life on that mountain yesterday— now—you—must bury them."

"There'll be better days," he said, and unhitched her horse. "You can ride double with me."

She agreed, and he put the wrapped dead men over her saddle and roped them down. It would be near dark before they reached the cabin. He wanted to be there. Cutter and Roland could help him dig the graves.

He rode stiff-jawed. She cried and alternately hugged him as they rode double for several hours. Riding up the meadow, he kept smelling whiffs of smoke. He halted Paint, and she asked him what was wrong.

"You smell hides burning?"

She nodded. "What would be the source?"

"I'm not certain."

When they topped the last ridge in the twilight, he saw the source of the smoke and reined up, not wanting to ride into a trap. The four walls of the collapsed cabin were a red rectangle of fire in the twilight down the valley below him.

"What—what's wrong?"

"The cabin's burning."

"Oh—who did that?"

He stared hard at the stark sight. "Renegades or outlaws."

"What outlaws would do that?"

"One called Red Dog."

"What can we do?"

"Get out of here till daylight, and then I can scout it when I am sure whoever done it is gone."

She fumbled with the saddlebag tie-down under her leg. "Here, I think we need another drink."

Numb with dread, he took the whiskey from her and stared at the burning shape. Where was Easter? What had happened to Cutter and Roland? Damn, this was a dead man's land. He uncorked the bottle and took a deep draught. He let it slide down his throat and recorked it. Better save some, he'd probably need it later.

8

Dog looked back over his shoulder expecting to see pursuit coming after them. He rode one of the dead men's horses at the rear, driving the herd hard. Mia was riding swiftly out in front, with the only mare on a lead and the mules on her heels. The other horses followed them in a hard run for the far timberline.

This would be the most dangerous crossing, with over two miles of open country to get over and no cover on the grassy basin. What they'd do for supplies—he wasn't sure about that. There was game to eat. His Indian ancestors had lived off the land before the white man came. No stores back then. Spurring his horse in close, he reached out and swung the quirt hard on the butt of a lagging bay horse. The pony sucked in his tail and shot forward. *Run, you lazy bastard, run.*

Another sneak look over his shoulder. He saw nothing. So no one had seen them and no one had trailed them from Cross Creek. There would be a posse this time. When they found that worthless Rube, who'd raped Dog's woman, smoking his own dick, they would get worked up and try to catch him.

Dog needed to cover their tracks. There'd be no way to do that and escape. But he'd figure out a way to throw them off if the posse came this far into the Big Horns. Maybe he'd even lead them to the renegades. Let those green bucks get the blame. He should have scalped those three back there. That would have really pointed the finger at those boys. With hooves thundering and horses heaving in the thin air, Dog closed in on the lodgepole thicket ahead.

He began to believe they'd make it undetected—

"Look!" Mia pointed to the north.

He saw the war party swooping down from the direction of snowcapped Soldier's Peak. Only one of the braves brandished a modern firearm. He carried a Yellow Boy and the brass shone in the mid-morning sun as he shook it over his head while charging wide open on his buffalo pony. The other two had bows. He knew he needed those two taken out first. The old rifle had little range and he doubted the boy's accuracy.

With his free hand he waved her on for the timber. Then he reached under the fender and came up with a Spencer repeater. The rifle in his hand, he swung his mount toward the chargers. If he couldn't defeat three boys, he deserved to die. He chambered a shell in on the move. He hoped the rifle had a full tube of bullets.

The war party was less than a quarter mile away, and they'd seen he'd turned out to fight them, so they'd turned more southerly to meet him head-on. When they cut that distance in half, he slid the horse on his heels to stop, dropped off, knelt, and took aim. His first shot took the screaming bow bearer on the right off his horse. With gun smoke in Dog's eyes, he whirled without a blink to take the left-hand one out. He put a bullet in the chest of his pony, and it skidded nose-down, piling the rider off. The rifleman, discovering he was the lone surviving warrior, reined up his horse in a hard skid with a strange look on his face. Before he could do anything, the horseless rider came running hard and in one bound was up behind him on the black piebald horse. They turned and fled.

Dog ran after them, firing the Spencer and calling them

cowards. They never stopped until they were gone from his sight. Out of breath, he bent over and shook his head. *Brave damn Sioux, those three.* He went to shoot the one lying on the ground. Standing over him, he dropped the rifle, jerked out his knife, then knowing this one was still alive, grasped a fistful of his hair and cut a circle on top of his scalp. The buck began to scream as Dog jerked the scalp lock loose.

"Tell them Red Dog scalped you. Tell them in camp!" he shouted over the howls in the face of the youth, who was holding his bleeding head and kicking his moccasins in pain. "Tell all of them Red Dog did this to you. Come after me again, the next time I'll scalp your crotch, balls and all."

Out of breath, he bent over to recover, grasping the greasy scalp in his fingers, the bloody knife in the other hand. He wanted this one to go back and tell them in the lodge circles that Red Dog, the breed, had scalped him. No bragging about how he saw the spirit or how he talked to the White Buffalo Goddess—but on the field of battle against three Sioux warriors, Red Dog single-handedly defeated us and scalped me.

Dog sheathed his knife, picked up his rifle, and went to where the white man's horse stood ground-tied. He jammed the rifle in the boot and swung into the saddle. Mia was already out of sight. Then, whistling "Gary Owen," which Custer's Band played at Fort Lincoln before they went to die at Sweet Grass, he rode for the timberline.

He knew the tune well. His mother whored with the soldiers at Fort Lincoln for money enough to feed herself. He had come by there looking for Snake before the Seventh Cav left Lincoln for their final battle. Weeks earlier, down at Fort Robinson, some Sioux women, drunk on Dog's whiskey, told him that Snake had gone up there to look for work scouting for Custer. But the fucking Crow hated Sioux breeds as much as they hated full-bloods, and the Crow told Custer's brother Tom not to hire Snake.

Custer might have lived too if he had hired Snake as one of his scouts instead of those lazy Crow. Yellow Legs deserved to die—that pious bastard riding around in buckskins with his long golden hair. After the Little Big Horn, the army said the Sioux had never scalped Custer. Lies for his pretty wife. Three years later, Dog had seen the unmistakable famous yellow scalp in a lodge one night when a drunk Sioux bragged to him how he'd completely skinned all of Custer's hair for his own prize. He dragged Dog to his lodge to show him the trophy. In the red light of the small tepee fire, the inebriated killer did a loud whirling stomp dance for him, shaking the whole scalp lock over his head.

"Custer, huh?" He shook the scalp in Dog's face. "You knew him?"

Dog nodded. It was Custer's all right. Then the next day the hungover Indian ran him down on the trail and offered him two ponies to forget what he'd seen the night before.

"Who would I tell?" Red Dog asked, knowing the ponies were good ones and the man had much to fear if the word got out he was the one that killed the golden boy. There were rich white men in Billings who would have put up a big price on this Indian's head to have him killed for scalping Custer.

"Oh, we are brothers," the Sioux moaned. "My wife and children are young. They need me."

"Cut your thumb," Red Dog ordered. This day he would have all the satisfaction.

The Sioux checked his hard-breathing horse and blinked at him. "You wish to be my blood brother?"

Hands on his saddle horn, Dog nodded affirmatively. It was one thing to bribe a breed, but a much greater shame to become his blood brother. This individual had become a high-ranking chief since the battle with the slaying of so many other leaders since the Custer fight.

The Sioux indicated the pair of prize paints. "I will give you those two horses."

"The three," Red Dog said, and nodded to the one the Sioux rode also. "And then we will become blood brothers to seal the deal."

The Sioux shook his long braids and acted insulted. He

squared his shoulders and turned the bald-faced pony around to leave.

"Is it two days' ride or three to Billings?" Dog shouted after him.

The Sioux reined up and turned back to frown at him. "Why do you ask?"

"They tell me there is little to eat on the reservation. You can buy a hungry man's soul for a few coins. If his babies cry in the night, would he not take silver and gold from a white man who wanted Custer's killer dead?"

"Yes—but your terms are too high."

"If you were dead, another young buck would fuck your wife as his slave and your children would be turned out for the wolves too."

The stiff wind came up through the waving grass. It was like the White Buffalo Snow Spirit whispered on the wind to the Sioux about his family's plight if he did not accept Red Dog's terms. At last, the Sioux nodded and stepped off his pony. Not because he wanted to did he use his skinning knife to slice his right thumb and hold it up. Not because he wanted to be a blood brother to a breed. But the alternative for him was even worse.

His jubilance restrained, Dog slipped off his pony to stand on his feet. This was a great day in his life. Perhaps his greatest victory. He drew his knife and made a cut from top to bottom of his thumb pad. With his thumb raised high, he pressed it against the Sioux's, and the older man clasped them hard together.

"Today—and forever, we are brothers," the Sioux said with authority.

"Yes, forever, we are brothers." There was no one to share this great event. They were alone on the vast rolling grass plains of South Dakota. Only the wind and a lone red-tailed hawk soaring overhead and screaming the news witnessed Dog's new standing among his mother's people.

Speaking of her, he'd found her earlier in Fort Lincoln in an alley under a drunken private. He'd battered the Polish soldier on the back of the head with a pistol butt and pulled him off her by his collar. She drew up her bare legs and hugged them, huddled in case he struck her too.

"Can you find no better man to screw than that foreigner?"

She shook her head and would not look at him.

"Here is some money—go home to your people." He threw some gold and silver coins at her.

"I have no people." She scrambled on her hands and knees to find the coins in the bad light behind the saloon.

"Listen to me!" he shouted in her ear, holding her up by the collar of her filthy leather blouse. She reeked of bad whiskey, horse sweat, and cum. "Go home. You no longer have a breed to suckle you. I am gone from your life. Go home."

When he dropped her in disgust, she fell on the ground like a hungry sow looking for spilled corn.

"Here," he said, and used his knife to slit open the soldier's pockets. More coins jingled out on the ground. Then, in his fierce anger, he straddled the unconscious soldier, turned the body over to expose his gray underwear and dirt-littered privates. Dog was poised to neuter him.

She grasped his knife arm. "No! No! They would blame me."

He shook loose of her. Then he sheathed his knife and went for his horse. He'd disowned her. His mother was dead.

That bitter night came back to him in a clear vision as he led his three new horses north in the too bright sunshine across the wind-flattened grass. He was blood brother to a great Sioux. His mother was dead.

In a short while, his mind and body were back in the Big Horns looking for Mia. He found the horses on the trail, then saw her standing, trembling and hugging her arms, wrapped in a gray wool blanket.

"All the horses here?" He stepped down in front of her.

She nodded dutifully, head bowed.

"What is wrong with you?"

"I feared they had killed you."

Stupid bitch. He reached out and took her by the back of

her braids, roughly shoving her down to her knees. "Those Sioux have all been taken care of. They ran off—"

He undid his gun belt and let it fall to the ground at his feet, then unbuttoned his pants before her face.

She knew what she must do. Red Dog smiled. Twice he had met his enemies and defeated them. Her warm mouth and hard tongue on his member relaxed his anxious muscles.

9

They made camp in the deep canyon. Slocum did not dare build a fire and attract anyone. He put feed bags with corn in them on the horses and mules. Lilly helped him as he explained they'd have to make sure they drew no attention to themselves.

"We can't let anyone know we're here," he said.

"Who all was at the cabin?"

"A young Shoshone woman named Easter and two cowboys. One was called Cutter and the other Roland. Neither of them were stupid about surviving. It may have been Red Dog and his men." He shook his head in disgust. "They're worse than most Indian renegades."

"You think they are all dead?" she asked as she put on the last feed bag. "The two cowboys and her?"

"Who knows? Come daylight, I'll scout things and see if there are any bodies."

"What will we do about . . ."

Struck hard by the realization of her loss, he caught her shoulder and hugged her tight to his chest. "I'm sorry, Lilly, I know today has been bad enough. You're a brave woman. We'll bury them too—in the morning."

"Oh, I'll be fine. I simply hope your friends are all right."

He shook his head and held her tight against his coat. The

74

sight of the burning cabin had told him the chances were not good that anyone had lived through the attack. At daybreak, he'd know for sure and decide what they needed to do. Get her out of the mountains and back to Cross Creek. At the moment in the cold night, that seemed the best plan he could devise.

He felt the worst dread over his responsibility to Easter. Why hadn't he taken her with him to Cross Creek? Because he'd thought she'd be safe with those two punchers. Damn, he should stop thinking.

"I'm not hungry," she said when he went to his saddlebag.

He leaned his forearm on Paint, who was busy chomping on the hard corn in the feed bag. "I'm not either, but I figured I could use a good jolt of whiskey."

"That sounds splendid."

He laughed and drew out the bottle. He uncorked it and handed it to her. "I have a cup."

"No." She raised the bottle in the starlight. "Here's to a better day tomorrow." And she took a deep draught of it. The liquor brought a deep cough from her.

He took the bottle and frowned in concern at her.

She put her hand on his chest. "I'll—I'll be—just fine."

"Good," he said, and tried the whiskey himself. It ran down his throat like a hot fire and warmed his eyes and ears, but when he paused before another swallow, he decided there was some relief in his tight muscles.

"I'll get what we have left to sleep under," she said, and started off before he could stop her.

He had been overgenerous in using two of their blankets on the dead men. He and Lilly would have to sleep together again or freeze.

"I never did that on purpose." He popped the cork back tight in the bottle with his palm and put it away.

"Yes, yes," she said, carrying the armload past him. "I figured that you did it on purpose."

"I never—"

She nudged him in the gut with an elbow while going by him. "I was only kidding."

He began to snicker, then he began to laugh. It wasn't the whiskey. It wasn't that funny. It was more like the laughter had been pent up in him all day and had to escape. Out of nowhere, she rushed over, tackled him around the waist, and forced him on his back on the ground.

Pinning his arms down, she struggled to hold him with some resolve. "I've wanted to do this all day."

"Why?" he asked, halfheartedly trying to escape her determined effort to pin him down.

"Why?" He raised his head to look at her.

"'Cause in some of the worst hours of our life I did this to Josh—" She fell on top of him and began to sob. "It always helped before—"

He held her tight, rocking her back and forth with the twigs poking him through the jumper. The worst hours of her life were being shared in a dark canyon with another man holding her like a bundled-up bear. Damn, things were in a big mess.

Before dawn he awoke, his arm over her, holding her against his body as he was curled around her. There was no way to disengage and not wake her. At least they had not frozen in the night, dressed in all their clothing under the remaining blankets. It was beginning to feel natural to sleep with her—something he needed to think hard about—she needed to be on a stage to Cheyenne. For sure not up in the Big Horns with killer outlaws and renegade Indians making life tough on everyone.

She raised her arm and pressed back against him. "You're like a big stove to sleep with." Then she raised up and looked at him. "That sounds bad."

"Not to me, and I'm the only one heard it."

She raised her blue eyes to the stars and then shook her head. She threw the blankets back and was getting ready to pull on her boots. "I guess I can tell all my friends in Texas I slept under the stars with the warmest fella I ever knew."

He was straining to get on his right boot while seated beside her. "They won't believe you."

She put on her second boot and elbowed him. "Why?"

"Not enough experience. I'm only the second fella you ever slept with."

"Hmm," she snorted. "Anyway, I won't tell them a damn thing about it."

"Yes, ma'am." On his feet, he jerked her up by one arm.

She put her hand on her lower back and winced. "You ever wake up sore from sleeping on the ground?"

"Every morning," he said, taking a Winchester out of the scabbard and filling his jumper pockets with .44/40 cartridges.

"I'm not staying here with the mules," she announced.

"Oh?"

"You go," she said, pointing to the slope above them, "I go."

"Grab some jerky. I'm fixing to head for the cabin."

She nodded as if satisfied. "Figured you'd argue with me."

He shook his head. "I'll know where you are this way."

"Oh, well," she said, and drew out some stiff jerky. "Is this really dried beef?"

"Supposed to be, but—"

She cut him off. "I don't want that answer. I'm ready."

At daybreak, they squatted on the ridge above the cabin and chewed the peppery jerky. Slocum saw nothing but the traces of smoke coming from the ruins. No sign of any of the other horses in the basin. No doubt they too had been taken in the raid.

Ready to start out, he reached over and clapped her on the leg. "There's some snow left on this side of the hill. Don't slip on it."

"I'll be careful." She wiped the corners of her mouth with a small kerchief. "Maybe I could tell all my Texas friends about the lovely food you serve."

"Oh, yes, they need to come up and eat off all my fancy dishes," he said over his shoulder as he started down.

"They must be old plates you found in an abandoned trunk. Have you ever been to San Antonio?"

He glanced back. "I would have been there right now if I hadn't run into Red Dog and his bunch. That detoured my return. Then a grizzly and a Shoshone maiden further held up my leaving."

"Oh," she said, stopping herself from falling by grabbing a lodgepole trunk. "Where do you stay when you're in San Antonio?"

He looked pained at her. "Not the same hotel you use, I am certain."

Holding the tree to regain her balance, she giggled. "I know where you must stay. Molly Michaels' Cat House?"

"Usually Ruby Sanchez's Cantina."

"Do they have clean sheets there?"

He paused and studied things again across the narrow basin. The big grizzly hide Easter had been tanning was gone from the stakeout on the south-facing slope. He held up a hand at the edge of the timber to stop Lilly.

"You better stay here till I look around."

"I'm lots tougher than I was yesterday."

He shrugged, not wishing to argue. So he waved her on, looking up and down the valley's trough as they hurried down across the small stream on rock islands and up the sharp bank to the cabin. Out of breath, they stood and recovered some a few yards away from the ashes and the stark blackened logs remaining.

He saw two forms on the floor under the collapsed remains of the roof. With care, he crossed the remains of the wall and went to the first one. When he bent down and rolled the blackened form over, he knew the first charred body belonged to Roland. He drew a deep breath; cooked flesh and clothing did not have a pleasant smell. Holding the kerchief to his nose, he moved over and squatted beside the second form. The remains of the plaid woolen shirt on the charred form belonged to Cutter. Slocum rose, sick to his stomach, and hurried to escape the acrid smoke and bitter fumes. Coughing hard, he came out like a blind man, stumbling away from the building, trying to regain his breathing and not puke.

She stiff-armed him to a stop on the edge of the steep slope to the creek. "Those men and her in there?"

"She ain't. They are—" He fell into a fit of coughing, and pushed her behind him as the surge of vomit erupted up his throat. The force bent him over and he vomited three times until he was at last having the dry heaves. Then he realized her hip was wedged against his, and the arm steadying him belonged to her as well.

"Can you sit down?" she asked. "I'll go get you some water."

He nodded and eased himself down to the ground on his butt. "I'd never have left them. I figured Red Dog hadn't followed me down here and those young bucks were only out for a vision."

"Vision?"

He nodded. "They come of age, they're supposed to go out in the wilderness on their own or with others their age and fast and find a vision that will help them through life."

"Who did this? Them?"

"I don't know. If I did, I'd feel better than I do right now."

"How is that?"

He started to stand and she kept him seated. "There is no rush. You get your stomach settled some. Then you can go look around for sign. I'll go get the horses and mules."

"What if you fall and break your leg going back?"

She looked around. "Since there is only you and me here," she pointed out, "then you will come up there and carry me down."

"Don't fall."

She rose and shook her head at him. "Great men at times need mentors. You are not a damn bit different than Josh was. I'll be back with the horses and mules in an hour."

He started to say something as she rushed down the slope on her boot heels. Instead, he waved her on. She looked back and shook her head as she crossed the small stream on rocks. He had to admit she was an attractive proper Southern woman. She looked like if she was ever tossed in the air, she'd always land on her feet like a cat.

He rose and went to find a shovel. There were some barefoot pony tracks around the yard and a moccasin print or two. But the arrows in everything told him enough. It was the *bear wounders* who had raided the cabin, killed the two cowboys, and kidnapped Easter—or whatever they'd done to the poor girl.

He kicked apart a pile of firewood at what had been the east end of the cabin and discovered a small shovel spared from the fire. Determined, he started to dig the first grave on the rise twenty yards west of the foundation. Earth never gave up many scoops of dirt without backbreaking labor. This ground did not disappoint him.

From time to time, he looked up at the hillside to the south, which was dotted with snow spots, and once he spotted her nearing the top in the trees. So nothing had happened to her—so far. After another half shovel of dirt and gravel thrown out, he was knee-deep in a narrow three-by-six grave. He never stopped. The sun reached near noon and he was wondering about her when he heard horses coming up the valley.

He reached for his rifle and climbed out. When he stood on the edge of the grave, he could see by all the hats that it must be a posse. Many of the men were dressed in suits and all carried long guns. Where was Lilly?

No sign of her in the crowd of men as they pounded up the valley. Someone noticed him above them on the rise. He shouted to the rest and guns came up. Wiser souls prevailed. The sheriff in the lead, his polished silver badge making a good target, scolded them and halted the posse.

He rode forward on a stout buckskin and nodded to Slocum. "Who died here?"

"Yesterday? Or two days before that?"

"Huh?" The sheriff's large black eyebrows formed a single line in his frown.

"Mrs. McCullem's husband and his foreman were shot and mutilated a few days ago over near Elk Creek," said Slocum.

"Oh, no. You found them?"

Slocum looked at the bleary-eyed posse members who were waiting for his answer, and he nodded. "We found their bodies yesterday. They'd been murdered and scalped."

"We need the army up here," someone said.

"Yeah, instead of sitting on their asses over there at the fort." Other complaints spread through the men on horseback.

The sheriff held up his hand for silence. "Who burned the cabin?"

"Same ones killed my friends Cutter and Roland." Slocum indicated the two bodies.

"That makes seven murders," the sheriff said with a grim set to his mouth and dismounted. "Rube Yarnell and his two sons were murdered and scalped outside of town."

"Renegades?" Slocum asked with a frown.

"There was a breed in town earlier flashing new gold double-eagles. He made a big order, left the store to supposedly get his pack animals, and never returned. We thought the Yarnells tangled with him. But one man couldn't have killed those three by himself."

"Describe him—this breed," Slocum said, feeling edgy about where Lilly was.

"Short, maybe five-seven. Reddish braids."

"A scar on his right cheek?"

The sheriff nodded. "You know him?"

"Red Dog. He's wanted in Montana for a stage robbery. Rides with a Sioux breed named Snake and a black calls himself Tar Boy."

"Maybe they helped him kill the Yarnells?"

"And made it look like renegades did it."

"Damn, I never thought about that." The sheriff shook his head as if upset. "Reckon they killed McCullem and his companion too?"

Slocum nodded. "That might explain the gold coins he had. McCullem, according to his wife, had lots of money on him from the cattle sale in Montana."

"Where is she, by the way? She came up here—"

"Riding right up the valley behind you." Slocum gave a nod in her direction as he saw her coming leading the pack animals.

"Oh, yes. Lovely woman," the sheriff said, and removed his hat.

Very lovely. Slocum gave an exhale of relief. She looked fine riding up on the sorrel.

"Gents," he said to get their attention as they all watched her. "I have four graves to dig. I'd sure appreciate some help."

"Sure," several replied. They didn't look at him, though. Lilly was the center of their attention and they all rushed over to help hold the leads, take the bodies of McCullem and his foreman, and fall over each other to impress her.

She directed the unloading of the supplies, the scrounging for firewood, the preparation of the campfire, and nodded to Slocum that she had matters in hand. "Food shortly."

Satisfied, he went up to the site of the grave digging. Two other small shovels had come from the posse's things. Dirt was flying like three badgers were at work. Slocum squatted down to observe, reminded of all the sore muscles in his back and ribs as another man used his tool to pry out the dirt.

"What happened to Davis?" the sheriff asked, joining Slocum. "This used to be his place."

"He was dead when I got here. A wounded grizzly got him the day before. I shot the bear and found a Shoshone girl here that Davis had kidnapped down on the Wind River."

The sheriff, Albert Hankins, a man in his forties with a full mustache that he needed to mash down with the web of his hand, nodded. "Where's she at now?"

"No sign or trace of her around here. The renegades must have her."

"Holy cow, Slocum, this business up here gets worse and worse the more I learn about it. You think that this Red Dog may have killed McCullem?"

"He got those gold coins somewhere and it wasn't by working. She said her husband had lots of money on him. He was a man who did not trust banks and usually demanded gold over paper money."

"Exactly," Hankins agreed. "You know where Red Dog's at?"

"Some cave or cabin, I'd bet, hiding out."

"That's a big order. It'll have to wait. I better check on these renegades, though. Maybe send them back home before they do cause problems. These town fellas don't mind one night away from mamma, but any longer, they get restless. What will you do?"

"Send Mrs. McCullem back with you once we have her husband buried, and then if you'll check on the renegades and try to recover Easter, I'll search for Red Dog. Maybe I can recover the money for Lilly."

"Renegades or someone killed them two." Hankins tossed a few clods at the bodies of the cowboys.

"I don't aim to be on that list."

Hankins nodded. "Neither did they."

Slocum agreed. Cutter and Roland had had no such ambition to be magpie bait either, that was for sure.

10

Red Dog decided the money belt felt uncomfortable to lie on as he studied the smoke coming from the low-walled cabin's rock chimney. He'd seen the white woman come out twice. Once, earlier, with a bucket to milk the yellow and white cow. Later, she fed the chickens who were scratching and fluffing themselves in dirt wallows around the place. At her first "Chick, chick" call to them, dusty red hens from four directions came on the run to peck at the scattered grain.

He studied the brown mesas and the junipers that dotted the valley. Less grass and drier down here, but a better place to winter than up in the high country. No man on the place—where was he? This might be ideal for them to hole up.

The horses she kept in the corral were work horses—not worth much. Her blue hound had scented him once or twice and bawled. His effort caused her to squint around at the surrounding country, but she didn't pay much more attention than that one good scan with her hand up for a shade from the glare.

Dog went back to his horse and rode to their camp. He dismounted and gave Mia the reins. Without a word for her, he went to the campfire and poured himself a cup of coffee,

Busy whittling on some red cedar with his jackknife, Tar

Boy, sitting cross-legged in the shade, nodded at his arrival. "You's learn anything down there?"

"Her man ain't there. Where's Snake?"

Tar Boy looked taken aback by the news. "Lordy, she's a Mormon widow."

"Huh?" Dog frowned at him over the steaming cup.

"Dey's puts their extree wives and kids out in places like that to run ranches and him have a new young wife at home to break in."

"How you know about that?"

Tar Boy rubbed the whisker bristles around his mouth and then showed his teeth in a big grin. "I learned all about it in Idee-hoe. Found me one of them widows. I cut her plenty of firewood. Helped her butcher and smoke two big hawgs. I even helped her mark some mavericks on the range."

"What did she pay you?" Dog asked, doubting his story.

Tar Boy grinned. "Aw, she done paid me every night lying on her back in that feather bed. Whew-ee, that was sure fine pay too."

Dog frowned at him in disbelief. "What happen when her husband come there?"

"I just stayed up in them hills. He only come by once a month, and den he never stayed long."

"Why did you leave her then?"

"I don't know. She got real mad at me one day about sump'n and I just rode off. Boy, it made me sick for days too. You know you get use to having a big hard-on every day, it ain't easy to get over it."

"You ever go back?"

Tar Boy shook his head and scratched his kinky scalp. "Wasn't no need. 'Sides, I done stole three good horses from a rancher nearby after I left her and they knowed I done it. So I cleared out of Idee-hoe."

"I see. We need to sneak up and take this one. I don't care if you screw this widow to death. We'll use her place to stay this winter and when the grass breaks in the spring, we can go south to Arizona."

"What if her husband comes by?"

Dog used the side of his left hand to slide over his throat. Then he reached for the coffee cup. He finished it in time to watch Mia run back from unsaddling his horse.

"Fix us some food. We got work to do." He shot a glance at Tar Boy. "Go find Snake. We need to take her today. I'm tired of sleeping on the ground."

"You sure be in a rush." Tar Boy pushed off to go locate the breed.

Rush—he'd think rush. Maybe Dog would kick him good sometime. He'd've done it then, but he needed him to make sure nothing went wrong when they took over this ranch. Him and Snake both. If those dummies hadn't burned that cabin, they could have stayed up on Trooper's Creek—but they were so damn sure that Tom White was inside the cabin when it burned up and that he was dead. That Shoshone girl would entertain Snake for a while, even if she never talked. Not bad-looking, but Dog didn't trust her—she might be a witch. Let Snake screw her to death—but if she ever used her witchcraft on them or he even thought she did, he'd kill that bitch.

After they ate, Dog sat at the campfire, fretting that the money that White had stolen from him in Montana had burned up in the cabin. Then he felt the heavy belt around his waist and smiled. He'd hold that much out of their share too. They should have got that money off White first. No chance, they'd said. They'd jumped the girl going for water and the two men were holed up in the cabin.

Snake shot a lot of arrows around to make it look like the renegades did it. Pretty smart of them—it and the killing of them hunters all pointed to those dumb Sioux bucks he'd defeated the day before up in the high country. Good, they could take all the blame. In a few hours, Dog and the others would have a roof over their heads and a place to hide out.

"Hurry up," he shouted at Mia as she rushed around loading their mules.

They left their camp and rode south off the mountaintop into the canyon country. At sundown, they watered their animals in the Powder River near its source, crossed it, and headed for the isolated ranch. Sundown caught them moving in a long line.

Snake took point, and in a few hours they rested close to the woman's place on a small stream. Without a fire, they gnawed hard jerky, huddled under blankets, and said little.

"I'll catch her going to milk in the morning," Dog said, and the other two nodded in the starlight.

"The dog?" Snake asked.

"You can sneak down there tonight and cut his throat," Dog said, knowing what the breed wanted to do. Probably cook him. He'd never had any craving for dog meat, but Mia and Snake would eat every bite of it and suck the bone marrow. His mother would have joined them at the feast—maybe the white blood in him was the reason he'd never liked it.

He was grateful he'd be down there waiting to ambush her while they ate the blue dog for their morning meal. Maybe that woman'd have some real food—eggs, pork meat, bread. He'd have her fix him some. Yes, have a feast.

Snake returned an hour later dragging the dog's carcass behind him in the moonlight. As if shaken by an unseen hand, the dozing Mia awoke, rushed over, and they talked excitedly about their treat. Nauseated over thinking about it, Dog rose and told them he was going down there. They barely nodded to him, engrossed in hanging the carcass up to skin it. He shook his head at them and started down the path through the pearly pungent sagebrush toward the ranch. With the freshly sharpened skinning knife in the scabbard on his hip, he imagined how the woman would pale in desperate fear when he jumped her and held the blade to her neck.

He reached down and adjusted his half-hard dick. The biggest regret was he hadn't used it on Mia before he left. Maybe later she'd be in heat after eating that dog meat. A small smile curled his lips—*you white bitch, I'm coming for you.*

Squatted in the shadows near her front door, he wished for a blanket to ward off the breath of old man winter, so cold at this time of day. The moon was far in the west, and dawn had not brought its rosy lavender to the range in the east. He heard sounds of things hitting each other inside that tensed him to get ready. She must be stoking her fireplace or stove. He'd like to hold his hands out to such warmth.

His shoulders hunched over against the cold, he readied himself to spring on her back. Over and over in the night, he'd planned and replanned how he would take her. Then the door bolt sounded and he saw her slip out with a bucket on her arm and close the door.

Before she could turn back, he sprang up, had hold of her, and had his knife's edge laid on her throat. She sucked in her breath.

"Don't move, bitch, or you'll be dead."

"Yes," she managed.

"Open the door," he said. "We're going back inside."

"Yes. But I don't have any money."

He reached down with the hand around the front of her and squeezed her breast. "Who says I want your money?"

The door swung open and he saw no one. She swallowed hard in his grip, and stumbled some as he pressed his body to her back to force her to move inside the candlelit interior.

On his first inspection of the large room, he spotted the flames in the fireplace and herded her over there. On the braided rug before the hearth, he released her and told her to undress.

"But—but—"

He waved the knife in her troubled face. "Undress or I'll shred your dress."

His left hand shot out and grasped a handful of the sleeve top, and he sliced off a patch of the material and shoved it in her face.

She gasped and shrank away from him. "You're mad."

His eyes narrowed when she did not obey him. "No, I am half white, half red man. That makes me much worse than either."

"All right, all right," she said, and began fumbling with the buttons. The red highlights from the fire shone on her trembling fingers as she hurried to open them. Soon the snow-white skin on her chest was exposed, along with the breasts that were pointed with dark-ringed nipples puckered by the cool air despite the reflective heat.

He stared at her actions. Filled with impatience, he stepped in and jerked the top down to expose her breasts. When she tried to move back, he jerked her up close and holding her, rubbed her breast hard with his other palm and fondled it.

"Get that dress off!"

Red-faced, she cowered and hurried faster to obey. When she was naked at last, he pushed her backward toward the quilt-topped bed, ignoring her protests. After a final shove, she bounced her butt on the bed. Staring hard at her pale face, he unbuttoned his shirt, undid the money belt and hung it over a chair, then his gun belt, and toed off his boots.

"I'm going to enjoy you—squaw!" His pants down, he stepped out of them.

Then he pushed her down on the bed, felt for his erection with his other hand. It was ready to rip her apart. He climbed on the bed. Then he roughly raised and spread her thighs apart. She knew the drill. With a grin on his mouth, he moved between them and sent his aching hard-on into her gates.

All at once, she looked up at him in wide-eyed shock and disbelief.

"Why, damn, woman, you ain't even got all my dick in you—"

"We's sorry," Tar Boy said close to his ear. His words made gooseflesh pop out all over Dog's bare skin. "But you's ain't been fair to us. You's can have this wrinkle-bellied white woman. We's taking Mia, the money, and the hosses. Don't follow us either 'cause we's will sure 'nough kill you."

Then the white woman screamed and Dog's lights went out from some hard blows to his head.

11

Slocum blew the steam off the cup of coffee that Lilly brought him. The sun was about to set, and the deer shot earlier by one of the posse members was roasting over the fire. The men appeared to have that job under control. She squatted beside him.

"What are your plans?" she asked.

"The posse is going to try to find the renegades. I'm going after Red Dog if I can find him and try to get your money back."

She nodded. "Where will you ever find them?"

"They'll show up or I'll cut some sign."

"The sheriff is convinced that this Red Dog killed my husband and Blake."

"The money points that way." Slocum tried the coffee, but it was still too hot.

"I want to hire you to find this Red Dog."

"I planned to go recover the money if I could."

"Where?"

He rubbed his left palm on top of his leg. "He probably isn't far."

"Will he run now that he's killed the Yarnells?"

"These mountains are a better place to hide than to get out in the open. He keeps a squaw, so he's not liable to run off and splurge in some whorehouse in Cheyenne or Denver."

She laughed quietly. "Is that where robbers go?"

"Tom Purple and his gang spent the entire amount of their Union Pacific robbery in Norma Jean's place in four nights down in Denver's red-light district."

"And—"

"When they were broke, the Denver police came in and arrested them."

"Convenient, wasn't it?"

"Good business." He wrinkled his nose. "The police owed more allegiance to Norma Jean than they did to the Union Pacific."

"You will let me hire you to find his killers?"

"All that money may be gone." He looked over at her hard.

She raised her chin. "I have other money."

He shifted his weight to his other leg. "I meant, he's liable to blow it before I can catch him."

"Money is not the object. I want him to face the hangman for his crimes."

"After I get you back to Cross Creek—"

She shook her head in the dying orange light of sundown. "I'm not going back there until we have him."

He drew a deep breath, and the smell of the cooking meat and wood smoke filled his nostrils. Grateful they were at a distance from the posse members down by the fire, he phrased his words to convince her she couldn't go along. "This is serious business. It won't be nice or easy. It'll probably snow again in a day or two and this country will be locked up."

"Slocum," she said in a low voice, "I don't fear anything except going back home and knowing—knowing that Josh's killer is out there free."

He nodded for a long time considering her words. No way he'd convince her to wait in town. Staring hard at the dark timbered hillside, he finished the cup and beat it against his leg. "It will be a tough, dangerous business and I can't promise you any success."

"I trust you'll do all you can."

"That might not be enough."

She clapped him on the arm and rose to her feet. "It will be all I ask." Straightening, she took the cup. "Now that that is settled, I'll go help them make some biscuits. The venison will be done enough to eat soon." Standing above him and looking around, she hesitated. "Josh would have been happy to live up here. It's a good place for the graves."

"I'm glad it is," Slocum said.

"You know what will be the hardest part for me?"

"No."

"Telling the woman who raised him that he's gone."

"His mother?"

"No, Comanches killed her when he was three. His aunt, her sister Marge, raised him. But she was Mom to him."

A grim set to his lips, he nodded. "That will be hard."

She went to check on the cooking. He watched her move toward the fire; she'd never shed a tear all day with the burial. He knew she was holding it back like a great dam and one day it would burst. Then she'd have it resolved— maybe she'd resolve it when her husband's killers were caught.

At dawn, the sheriff rustled his grumbling army out of their bedrolls for coffee, more venison, and biscuits. The bleary-eyed posse members huddled under blankets in the cold, eating and swilling down the hot Arbuckle's finest. The valley sat painted silver with a hoary frost, and the men's breath came out in great clouds.

One man, watering his horse, slipped and fell lengthwise into the small creek. After much laughter, they soon had him undressed and wrapped in blankets and his clothing drying at the fire. Saddles were tossed on the mounts, and a few of the horses bucked around under their riders. Hat-waving men still on foot herded the buckers, shouted, and laughed at their cohorts' plight.

On his stout horse, Sheriff Hankins, after flattening his mustache with the web of his hand for the sixth time, scowled at it all. "Anyone ain't in the saddle in two minutes is going to be left behind."

He reined around and spoke to Slocum. "Guess you'll show her back to town?"

"I can't talk much sense in her. She wants to run down the killers."

The sheriff looked displeased. "Hell, she ought to know better'n that."

"She's had a big loss. I'll look out for her."

"I guess you have so far." Hankins lowered his voice. "I'd rather have her with me than this whole bunch."

Slocum grinned, reached up, and shook his hand. "You going to look for the renegades over east where I saw their camp?"

"Try. You be careful. That breed, I figure, by hisself killed all those Yarnells, and they weren't Sunday-school teachers either." He checked his horse.

"I will. You look out for that Shoshone girl Easter. If you find her, make sure she gets a good start back, you know what I mean?"

Hankins agreed with a firm nod and waved his arm over his head. "Let's ride. Daylight's burning."

The posse short-loped up the eastern slope, following Slocum's directions to where they had been camped earlier. He watched them climb the hillside for the ridge. Some horses still acted unruly with their riders fighting with them. Satisfied, he turned back to the fire where Lilly was packing up.

Two posse members had stayed with a third one, the man who was drying out from his fall in the creek. Obviously, they'd had enough playing lawman, and were helping Lilly reload the panniers before they headed for home.

Slocum tossed the saddles on their two horses and cinched them up. Then he rolled up their bedrolls, grateful for the extra blankets some of the posse had given them. Even with the added cover, it sure wasn't as warm sleeping by himself as it was with her. But for the sake of respectability, they'd slept apart.

"Where will we go next?" she asked, meeting him coming down to the fire leading the saddle animals.

"There has to be some sign that Hankins missed. I think they went south and may have moved into the lower Big Horns."

"What's down there?"

"Some riffraff wanted by the law somewhere. And some Mormon widows."

"Widows?"

"Not really. But that's a nice name for discarded wives. Their husbands put them out there to watch after some range cattle and scratch a living out of some creek bottom while they live with the newest young wife over in Utah."

"Polygamy?"

"Yes. They say there's a way a man on the run can easy-like slip down the spine of the Big Horns, cut over into Green River country and down into the Arizona Strip, and make his way to Mexico. There's plenty of those small remote ranches to stay at for a few coins."

"Will Red Dog go that way?"

"I don't figure he's looking for a home coming back up in Montana unless he's willing to risk a lynching party. With the money he took, all he wants to do is keep his head down and get the hell away."

"So where do we start?"

"He has a good head start and we might—"

"Might what?"

"Take a big step and cut straight off in that direction and see if he's shown up down there." He pointed south with his forefinger.

"And if he hasn't?"

"We can always come back to the high country and search every cabin and cave."

She agreed. "You mentioned winter coming on."

"We'll cross that river when we get to it."

"Fine, you're in charge. The mules are loaded. I'm ready."

"Let's go." Slocum turned to shake the remaining posse

men's hands and thanked them before he stepped up on Paint and he and Lilly headed south.

She looked around as the rising sun heated them. "I spent my honeymoon on a pack trip."

"Where to?"

"Josh took me to his ranch in the hill country. It was fun and we had only one brush with the Comanche along the way. We about rode right into a war party in a deep canyon. It was too close. We hid in the live oak until they went past." She smiled slightly. "But I still like the adventure of a pack trip."

By afternoon they were winding down into the broken country of junipers and mesas. The ridges were roached with lodgepole pines and the valleys with cottonwoods that still wore their coats of golden leaves. The afternoon sun's slanting warmth forced them to shed their coats.

"No one live around here?" she asked as they rode beside a silver stream that one could easily leap over.

"A few trappers like Davis. And some Mormon widows are scattered out south of here."

"How many widows?"

"Not over a handful—three or four, and they're so scattered out on separate ranches and so far apart, they can't even get together."

"What do they do if they get sick or—" She turned her palms up as they rode.

"I've heard two of them say they've had babies by themselves."

"Oh, no—"

"Hey, all I've done is passed through here." He turned and saw the flicker of rider and horse on their back trail. No hat—

She laughed aloud at his words—he stuck his hand out with a frown to silence her.

"What's wrong?" she hissed, and her eyes cut around to see what was wrong.

"Don't look back, but we've got company."

"Who?"

"I suspect those renegades. Head this pack train for that grove. I'll be beating their butts."

She put spurs to her sorrel and he moved in to spook the mules. They began running and honking. Hooves pounding the short grass, they swept down the valley. As Paint crowded the mules, Slocum drew his Colt and twisted in the saddle. Three war-painted bucks were sweeping off the steep hillside with bows and arrows. A fourth one was directly behind. He sent an arrow past Slocum that thudded into the pack without doing damage. In reply Slocum shot at him twice, and the buffalo pony spooked sideways, dropping his rider off in a tumble. One down.

The grove drew closer and the mules were running hard with Lilly. But they were still some distance away, an eighth of a mile. She turned the sorrel and mules off into the creek in a great splash, then up the far bank with Slocum close behind, worrying about the other two renegades.

"You're doing great!" he shouted.

Grim-faced, she nodded at him and kept on riding. They slid to a halt amid the gnarled trunks of the ancient cottonwoods. He holstered his Colt and slipped the rifle out as he stepped down.

On his knee, he took aim and put the center blade of the sight on the piebald horse of the lead renegade coming out of the water and cresting the low bank. He pulled the trigger, and the black and white pony broke his stride and fell sideways into the path of a bald-faced bay. The collision threw both riders off their mounts. The third one reined up and swung around. Slocum's next shot missed him.

"Here," she said out of breath, and handed him her rifle. "I'll reload that one."

He accepted it and nodded. "I've got to go get them before they recover. You stay low."

"No—"

He was already gathering the reins. While they were undecided, he needed to take them if he could. In the saddle, he gave her a sharp nod. "Get under cover."

Then he slapped Paint on the butt with his rifle to get him turned around. It was do or die in this valley. He had no intention of dying. Screaming like a banshee, he headed for the two, who were crossing the creek on foot to escape his wrath.

The dog slumped down to the sod, whimpering, then managed to rise. Stunned, it tried to get its tongue while, He had to do it quickly to escape, screaming like a banshee. He headed for his tent. He never breathed the word "break in escape."

12

Red Dog's head felt like a busted pumpkin. Still groggy, he found himself facedown on a dirt floor. Acrid dust filled his nostrils. He was also tied up. His body felt so cold he shivered, realizing then that he had no pants on and his bare legs and butt were exposed. Where in the hell—

"I see you done woke up," a woman's sharp voice suddenly said.

He tried to roll over and see her, but as bound up as he found himself, that was not possible. He was frantic to get loose, and his thoughts were in a whirlwind. What should he do next?

"Well, a cat got your tongue?" she demanded.

"No."

"I should'a kilt yeah. Nerve of you, breaking in here and raping me."

He never answered her.

A swift kick to his kidneys made him grunt. "Who was that black and breed come in here and robbed you anyway?"

"Tar Boy and Snake."

"They's gone."

'Where?"

"How the hell would I know? They left. They're your friends, ain't they? If your kind ever has any friends."

98

"They work for me."

He heard her pull out a chair behind him.

"They did," she said. "How much damn money was in that dang belt anyway?"

"Don't know."

"You mean you didn't know how much money you had? Lord, I can tell you to the penny how much I have."

He raised his head up to relieve the kink in his neck, still unable to see her because she was behind him. "How much?" he asked.

"Seventy-three cents."

"How come so much money?"

"Ain't none of your damn business." She kicked him in the shoulder with her bare toe.

"How did you earn that out here?"

"A cowboy rode by one day a few weeks ago. He said he was near broke and out of work, could he trade me some labor for a meal and letting him stay overnight. I said sure. I don't get much company."

"And?" Straining at his binds had done nothing to make them looser. His efforts only cut the cords deeper into his skin.

"Aw, he split stove wood, and a pile of it too. He was a hard worker. I fed him. He kept looking at me. You know how a man looks at a woman when he's been out sleeping with the dry cows for months?"

"Yeah."

"I said how much money you got? 'Seventy-three cents.' Fair enough, give it to me."

"He did?"

"Yeah, he did." And she laughed. "Stayed three days and I have enough stove wood to do me six months. But you're different. Guess I should've kilt you right off when them two left you."

"How long they been gone?" He closed his eyes in disgust over his dilemma.

"Since morning. It's mid-afternoon now. I begged 'em to take you along."

"What did they say?"

"That black one, he said no. They was fixing on moving fast. I can't for the life of me figure why they left you alive anyway. They knowed sure as sin you'd follow 'em for all that money."

Dumb, they were both dumb. He sneezed from the dirt and drew his body up in a ball. "Untie me."

"I untie you and you'd overpower me. No, sirree, you're all right on the ground right now."

"I'll give you half the money." He squeezed his eyes shut to close out the chill.

"I ain't stupid. You probably double-crossed them two."

"No, I came to take over your house for a hideout and we were going to stay here all winter."

"Stay here all winter?"

"Then when spring came, we'd go to Arizona. You ever been there?"

"My sister lives at St. David."

He had no idea where the hell that place was at. "We get that money back, we can go down there."

"Why would you need me?"

"Can you count?"

"Sure."

"Can you read?"

"All those books over there plus the Bible and the Book of Mormon and lots more."

"You asked why I didn't know how much money I had."

"Hmm, if it was so much—"

"I can't count or read. We'd make good partners. You do all that stuff and I'd do the rest."

"Rest?"

"Yeah, you'd be sure they don't cheat us—you know."

"Yeah, I'd untie you and you'd fly away like a wild goose and I'd be lucky if you didn't kill me before you left."

"I swear—"

"Swear to what—you ain't got any religion." He heard her sigh and stand up. "I got eggs to gather and a cow to milk.

Maybe after that I can figure out what in the hell to do with you."

He didn't answer her. While she was gone doing that, he'd get loose—somehow.

He watched her dusty dress tail, the hem raveled from dragging in the dirt, and saw the bare soles of her feet pass him and go out the door.

"Don't you go nowhere," she said, and closed the door after herself, shutting off the cold blast that swept over him and chilled him deeper. His shoulders even quaked, he felt so chilled to the bone.

Somehow he had to convince her to be his partner and get her to untie his binds. No use straining, he was tied too well with fresh rope. The binds only cut deeper in his wrists and ankles. If he ever caught Tar Boy and the others—he might cook and eat them all three. Mia especially for going along with them. Why, she'd have been starving over in South Dakota on the reservation if he hadn't taken her in. The ungrateful little bitch.

How did Tar Boy get Snake to go along on the double cross? Why, that blanket-ass breed would have died outside Fort Lincoln from drinking bad whiskey if Dog hadn't gone up there and rescued him. Custer never would have taken Snake to the Little Big Horn. Greed got them two. Greed might get her to untie him. He needed to work on it.

The door creaked open and the fresh north wind washed over him. He met her blue-eyed gaze as she swept inside with a milk bucket in one hand and a wicker basket in the other.

"You ain't gone nowhere," she said, and whisked by him.

When she was out of his sight, he strained on the ropes behind his back. His left arm was asleep with pins and needles underneath him. He wondered if it would ever work again.

"That ole cow is going dry," she said. "Them hens are too. I only found three eggs. Must be these shorter days, huh?"

"I don't know about cows and hens."

"You mean you ain't a farmer?"

"No, I'm not a farmer."

"You know about Mormonism?"

"No."

"Well, see, you get you some wives and you make them farm for you while you lay up with a new one."

"I see."

"No, you'd like that. Most men do."

"I like money. Those two have it. Let's get it back."

"Me and you against them two mean hombres?" She made a pained face.

"They ain't that tough or they'd've taken me face-to-face. They waited till—we were doing it."

Obviously, she was straining the milk through cheese-cloth behind his back. He could clearly smell the strong whang of hot raw milk and heard it pouring into a vessel.

She cleared her throat and scowled down at him. "You were raping me."

"Your husband do that to you?"

"Yes, but I am his to rape whenever he wants it."

"I did it 'cause I thought you were pretty and had to have you."

"Same reason he does," she said. "He gets horny."

"No—I thought you were pretty undressing for me."

"Oh—I should have kilt you. Now—now I can't. But I know you're lying—lying to me."

"We will go to Arizona and see your sister."

"How many people you killed already in your life?"

"What's that got to do with you and me?"

"How many?"

"Not enough."

"Not enough?"

"I said that. They all needed killing and some others did too."

"'Cause they got in your way—right?"

"No, 'cause they stole my money!" He gritted his teeth and strained at the ropes. Particles of grit ground on his molars from the floor dust and he tried to spit them away. It only ran down the side of his mouth. Damn, if he ever got loose, he'd strangle this bitch with his bare hands.

"I may just leave you here. Hiram, that's my husband, will never believe all this happened out here. I figure you'll kill me and then go kill your so-called friends and get that money."

"No, I said—" He lowered his voice and raised his head up to hear her better. "I'd take you to Saint Whatever."

"St. David." She snorted. "It never snows there. That's what she said. Never snows. Never gets real cold."

"I'd like to live there with you."

"Me get a divorce from Hiram, huh?"

"Sure, I get that money back, we can afford that." He looked up at the open shake ceiling for answers on how to convince her. "I'd marry you and hire some Messicans to do all the work."

"How much money was there anyway?"

"Hundreds, thousands." Tired of holding it up, he dropped the side of his head on the hard floor. "More money than you could count in a day."

"I can count fast."

"Not that fast. They are getting away with it."

"Guess you'd buy me a new dress or two."

"I would. I would. Fanciest dress in St. David with lace and all that."

"How will I know I can trust you?"

"You said you had two choices. Kill me or turn me loose. You said you can't kill me, so turn me loose."

"How good's your memory?"

"Real good."

She was squatted on the floor in front of him holding a sharp-looking knife. The sight of that blade made his scrotum shrivel up tighter than the cold air had. No telling about a madwoman. He knew a buffalo shooter at Dodge that got drunk once and beat up his woman like usual. Later, when he passed out in the night, she used his own skinning knife on his bag and left him a gelding. What was this woman's purpose?

"List what you promised me. Go ahead." She cut an impatient gaze at him.

"To—ah, marry you—"

"After you pay for a divorce." She slapped the side of the knife blade on her other hand to keep time with each word.

"Yes—yes, after I pay for the divorce, I'll marry you and we'll go to St. David and I'll buy you a big house and hire lots of help. And—and I'll buy you dresses. And it never snows there."

Had he convinced her to cut him loose?

13

"Halt!" Slocum fired his rifle at their heels.

They jumped in the air to escape his bullets and turned, looking pale under their war paint. Hands high, they obeyed him, looking at one another as if to ask how this could happen.

"What did you do with the Shoshone Indian girl?"

The short, fatter one answered. "We do not have her. Who is she?"

"The one at the trapper canyon."

"We don't have her." They spoke quickly among themselves in Sioux. All of them held out their empty brown palms and shook their heads.

"Black man and breed have a woman with them," the fat one said.

Damn, they must have her. Slocum sat the anxious Paint, checked him with a tug on the bit, and considered his prisoners—they knew more than they were telling him. "You killed two hunters."

The fat one shook his head with a serious look on his dark face. "Black man and two breeds do that too. We never kill them."

Filled with disgust, Slocum scowled at them. "Then why in the hell were you after me and her?"

"Need horses to go home. Need supplies."

"What about your quest?"

Fat Boy looked at the ground in defeat and shook his head. "We never find it here. White eyes have spoiled this land too."

"Now you have one horse to ride home. What do you have to eat?"

"This horse." Fat Boy indicated one that Slocum had shot.

"I think you better start for home. You're lucky that posse didn't find you. They would have hung all of you." Slocum knew how much Indians hated the thought of being hung.

"How can we go home on foot?"

"Travel at night to the Powder River, then skirt the Black Hills. Once you reach the badlands, you'll be home free. Don't kill or attack anyone, or the army will sure find you."

Fat Boy spoke to the others in Sioux. His words made them all look at their moccasins for answers. Then they began to nod in agreement.

"You know if that black man or the breed has the Shoshone woman?" Slocum asked Fat Boy.

He turned and nodded. "It is the breed with him that has her. The one they call Snake. There are three of them and two women. We don't know the third one."

"Red Dog," Slocum said. "Where are they now?"

"Rode south." Fat Boy used his flat hand to show their direction of travel.

Slocum nodded. "What're you going to do?"

Fat Boy looked displeased that he had asked. "Go home."

"That's good. I won't kill you then."

Fat Boy's brown eyes widened and he looked at Slocum in disbelief.

Slocum checked Paint again with his left hand and pointed the Winchester at the Sioux for effect. "I came up here to kill all three of you. You understand that?"

Fat Boy said something in Sioux to the others and they nodded in defeat.

"It ain't a good day to die or a good place. The gods might not find you. Go home. Leave no footprints."

"What is your name?" Fat Boy asked.

"Slocum."

"You are a good grandfather, Slo-cum. We will use your wisdom and go back to our lodges."

Wind ruffled Paint's short mane. Slocum checked his impatience and nodded to them. "May you live for the embrace of your own people."

"Ho," they answered, and Slocum short-loped back to the cottonwoods and Lilly.

She rushed out leading the mules and sorrel. "Are you all right, Slocum?"

"Fine," he said, and stuck the rifle in the scabbard, looking back to observe that the three had gone to see about the dead horse.

"What about them?" she asked.

"I think I talked them into going home. It was either that or kill them, and I wasn't in the mood to do that."

"Will they follow us?" She looked warily in their direction before she mounted her horse and jerked up the mules' heads from grazing.

"No." He gave a sigh and looked back toward the renegades. "I think I have them convinced to go home. They're a little defeated and depressed. They came up here to find a high spiritual experience and have failed."

"Learn anything else?"

"They said that Red Dog and his men killed your husband, and they also killed Cutter and Roland and have Easter."

She nodded. "Then we are on the right trail?"

"Yes, Lilly, but those three will be lots tougher to take than these kids. Let's ride."

They made camp beside a stream he had no name for. With a fishhook and some string tied on a willow baited with worms, he caught four small cutthroat. Meanwhile she made bread in the Dutch oven. With the fish frying and biscuits baking, they sat cross-legged on a blanket and sipped fresh coffee in the twilight.

On the ridge above them, a throaty wolf howled for the

moon to come up. His mournful voice went unanswered as Lilly scooted closer to Slocum.

"They can sure make the gooseflesh run up my spine."

"Not much danger of them bothering us. They've got game to chase, and only in desperate times do they ever bother with humans."

"Still—" She moved forward on her knees to turn the fish in the bubbling fat. The done sides of the trout were a crisp brown in the fire's rosy light. "I don't like wolves."

"I guess there's got to be wolves in this world. Like there's outlaws, makes you appreciate the better things."

She laughed and settled back beside him. "You're perfectly comfortable out here, aren't you?"

"Sure, got lucky. Caught some fish. And I have the company of a lovely lady to share this meal."

"I don't know about that. But this is your home out here, isn't it?"

"Sometimes."

"No, you live easy out here. Places like this are your home. Inconveniences don't bother you, do they?"

"It depends."

"On what?" She swept the hair from her face and tied it back with a ribbon.

"I can't explain it. Times I love to be down on the square in San Antonio. Basking in the sun, drinking good mescal, and talking with people I like to share the day with, but there's always someone lurking over my shoulder in the shadows. I am never totally safe there. Here I seldom have a problem."

"I see. But you need so little. Josh would have built a lean-to and gone to all kinds of preparation. I'm just not used to your easygoing ways—I don't mean it upsets me. It's much less frantic." Then she laughed and reached over to clap him on the arm. "Thanks for putting up with a silly woman."

"No problem. How are those biscuits?"

"Probably real brown. I am intoxicated by this country and all." She struggled up to get her hook and lift the Dutch oven lid for inspection. "Done. Not burned either."

"I'll put the fish on the tin plates and we can eat."

"Wonderful." She spooned out some steaming bread, and he handed her a plate with two fish on it in exchange for two biscuits.

They ate their supper as the stars began to spray the sky. An owl hooted and their horses shuffled in the dense silence, accompanied by the creek's soft music. The meal completed, they washed their dishes in the stream and headed back to the glow of the fire.

"It'll be cold tonight," he said.

"Yes, it was last night. I am rather spoiled from having your warmth, if that is not too forward."

"No, ma'am, I feel the same."

"We better turn in then."

"Sure," he said, and went to check on the animals. They were asleep, hitched on a picket line strung between two trees. He went past a gnarled trunk and emptied his bladder. He wondered about Easter and how they were treating her. If they'd hurt her . . . he'd beat the living hell out of 'em. Afraid that they might have hurt her, he shook his head. No way that bunch treated anything right. His pants rebuttoned, he went back and stoked the fire.

"Anything wrong?" she called out from the bedroll.

"No, just checking." He brought the rifles over and set them close by.

"Expecting trouble?" she asked from under the covers.

"No, but I'm still not taking chances."

"Good, then I won't worry."

He toed off his boots, removed his jumper, and undid his holster. He wrapped it up and put it close by where his head would be, then climbed under the soogans. On his back, he looked at the stars. Must have been ten million of them.

She reached over and squeezed his hand. "I like your ceiling."

"It ain't bad," he said, and rolled over on his side. Soon he was nested against her back. He put his arm over her, hugged her to him, and felt a little heady. Lots of woman there—her husband must have really enjoyed her—damn sure not whiny about anything either.

The mules pitching a fit awoke him. He scrambled to pull on his cold boots.

"What's wrong?" she hissed.

"Horse thieves it sounds like." He picked up his six-gun. "Stay low."

He ran for the picket line, hearing pounding hooves leaving. If he only could stop them—that had to be those boys. Damn their mangy hides. In the moonlight, he saw them in the distance leading off the two horses. Too far off away already to bother to shoot at them. He stuck the Colt in his belt and rushed about gathering mule leads. Obviously, the mules had an aversion to Indians or they'd have gotten them too.

Those sonsabitches weren't going to walk home after all. He stomped his foot. Blast their rotten hides anyway.

"What did they get?" she asked, out of breath as she ran up to hug his arm.

"Your sorrel and Paint."

"Why not the mules?"

"They had a fit and didn't want to go."

"Really?"

"Mules aren't dumb. Ornery and cussed mean, but they're probably smarter than horses."

"Can we ride them?"

"After daybreak I'll try them out. They've been packed enough they should ride, but that's not a guarantee."

"It was those Sioux boys, wasn't it?"

"I'm certain it was them. You heard them kyacking like coyotes leaving here, didn't you?"

"Yes."

"It was them all right. I regret not leaving them dead for the magpies." He double-tied the mules. "Let's get some sleep. Morning will come soon enough."

"Tomorrow?"

"That's coming, let's sleep awhile."

"Josh would have been up all night planning his revenge." She hung on his arm as they went back to the bedroll.

At last, when they were settled back under the covers, she

raised up, bent over, and kissed him. She swept her hair back and smiled. "Thanks, you're a neat guy."

He snuggled over on his side. "Not neat enough to ward off rustlers."

She backed into him and laughed. "No way you can stay awake all night."

"I should have been more alert."

She reached back and patted his leg. "Go to sleep."

While she made breakfast the next morning, he saddled the mules. They stomped a lot and acted up, but they did that on a regular basis. He decided to try One Ear first, so named because a portion of his right ear was missing. Perhaps bitten off by a man earring the mule down in his earlier life.

In the saddle, holding the reins out and booting him with his heel, Slocum spoke to One Ear. After some hesitation, the mule finally stepped out like he was walking on eggs. Slocum rode him around in circles and discovered he didn't rein good, but never offered to buck. He felt satisfied One Ear would do for Lilly. Braying and dancing around the tree on his tether, Phillipe, the other jackass, was upset to be separated from his buddy.

She called Slocum to breakfast. He dismounted close by and retied his mule to a tree with rope, not trusting the reins. After washing his hands in the creek, he flung them dry in the cold air and joined her. He accepted the tin cup of steaming coffee.

"Maybe we should go back to Cross Creek and get more horses?" she asked.

"Aw, the mules will do. That trip back there would put us five days further behind them."

"I'm with you."

"It won't be as easy riding mules, but if they keep heading south, I bet we can buy some horses off those ranchers on the way."

She dished him out some fried potatoes and biscuits on a tin plate. "How much of this foodstuff and gear will we need to leave here?"

"I guess the Dutch oven and those things. We can tie on

the coffeepot and one frying pan, then make us a few small sacks of coffee and food. That and our bedding is all we can pack out. One Ear acts like you can ride him."

"I think I can do that while you ride Phillipe."

He scratched his sideburns and shook his head. "Sorry, it won't be handy."

"Eat. I don't need it handy. I want those killers."

"Yes, ma'am." He sat with his plate near the small fire and absorbed the heat on his face. They needed to be down in lower country. A big snow could sweep out of Canada down the spine and bury them here.

"And quit the 'yes, ma'am.' We aren't that formal."

He chuckled. "All day on that mule and it will be formal."

"They are that bad?"

He held half a biscuit ready to pop in his mouth. "They don't neck-rein and they can be hard to manage."

"Only a small bump in the road."

He glanced over at her and shook his head. When sundown came, she'd sure know all about mules.

14

She held out his pants to him as he sat on his bare butt. He rubbed his wrists where the rope had cut deep into skin and left them raw.

"Here, put them on."

He nodded and started to get up. "What do they call you?"

"Alma."

"My name is Dog, Red Dog."

"Fine. How you got that name, I'll never know."

He pulled the pants up. "An Indian gets a name from what his parent sees outside the lodge. She saw a red dog. How do white people do it?"

"They get lots of names out of the Bible."

"I would call you Pretty Water."

She shrugged as if uncomfortable about his attention. "Call me whatever. I'll dish you up some mush." With that said, she started for the fireplace.

"Those horses in the barn—we can ride them?"

"They're broke." She bent over and used a wooden spoon to fill the bowl from the iron kettle.

He was behind her, and rubbed his hands on the dress material over the sides of her hips. Hesitating to straighten up, she cleared her throat. He took a half step back and his arms encircled her waist. With his mouth close to her ear, he whispered, "I meant what I promised."

Frozen in place, she nodded. "You better eat first—"

His hands cupped her firm breasts under the thin dress and he closed his eyes as he pressed against her firm butt. The sweet musk of her body filled his nose. The soft curly hair was in his face as he nibbled on her ear. Half-drunk with passion's desire for her body, he knew she could feel his growing erection between them.

She hunched her shoulders under him. "I guess there is more mush." Then she began unbuttoning the dress. "You have greater needs than food—obvious—ly."

His hands soon squeezed the flesh of her pear-shaped breasts. His mouth worked on the smooth skin of her neck and he soon explored the slight swell of her belly, and she sucked in her breath when his fingers combed through her curly pubic hair.

She led him to the bed and shrugged off the dress. Carefully, she laid it across a chair as he swiftly undressed. On her butt, she moved under the covers and soon lay on her back, her arms out to receive him as he climbed in with her. On his knees between her legs, he hauled the blankets over his back and then drove his rock-hard erection in her.

With her legs wrapped around him, he sought the depth of her cavity and smiled. He never thought he'd ever have a smooth-skinned white woman in bed with him that was not repulsed by him being a breed. How many white whores had said they didn't fuck Injuns and turned away from him? He remembered the haughty golden-haired one in Lost Camp who told him that and then stalked off. How he later caught her alone and put his knife to her throat, dragged her into a stall. Then he showed her how Indians raped such white bitches in the horse shit. But this was different—Alma was breathing hard with his every poke. Her head was tossing in pleasure and her eyes were glazed. And her rock-hard clit was scraping his shaft like a nail. This was better than all the rest. She was even contracting inside and raising her butt off the bed to meet his force. In the whirl of their heated fire, he felt himself coming and shoved his dick hard into her. She clutched him tight. He'd never came so hard—his balls shriveled and he came again and again.

"What about the money?" she asked in a drunken slur.

He raised himself on his stiff arms over her. "Who cares?"

Then they both laughed as he dropped down and began feeding on her breasts.

In the dawn's weak light, Dog felt hungover from the night before with its fierce repeated copulations as he saddled the two thin bays and led them to the house. When they were hitched at the rack, he went inside to get the bedroll she'd made of her blankets. He nodded to her, took it outside, and put it on the horse she would ride. Then he took out her canvas war bag and hung it on the saddle.

The only gun Snake and Tar Boy had overlooked was her small-caliber .25/20 Winchester repeater. A center-fire cartridge that would kill deer in close range and varmints, but not a long-range weapon. Still, it was better than a bow and arrow—besides, she had a new box of shells for it. He wondered how far they'd gone, Snake, Tar Boy, and Mia. No telling. He'd run them down. Not many places to spend that money between there and maybe Arizona.

In a few minutes, she came out, closed the door. She wore a divided skirt, button-up Sunday shoes, and a black wool coat. Her reddish hair was tucked under a felt hat with a rawhide string to keep it on. She mounted and nodded tight-lipped at him. Time to go.

They had enough provisions not to starve if he shot some game. They simply needed to find those three—four, counting Snake's Indian woman—if he hadn't grown tired of her and left her for dead somewhere.

The sun rose and shone on the blanket he used for a coat, but offered little heat. Their horses' unshod hooves stirred up acrid-tasting dust. Dog could easy enough see the imprints of the two-day-old tracks headed southwesterly. The thin ponies he and she rode wouldn't last many days of hard pushing. He needed to be on the lookout for others. Maybe they'd find some range horses—without money he'd have to steal them.

The notion of being penniless only made him madder. Once or twice she rode in close and put her hand over on his leg, squeezed it, and smiled at him. He nodded his approval in return, but her slight caresses gave him an erection every time. He had not been this easy to arouse since he was a boy.

Late that afternoon, they approached a small ranch and she said she knew these people.

"Would they have better horses?"

"I don't know—"

"Would they trust you to pay them later for them?"

"If not—I have a gold ring."

He nodded, impressed that she would part with her gold ring for him. "They must be good horses to do that."

"I understand."

"What will they think—I mean about us?"

She drew her shoulders back and frowned. "None of their damn business."

He chuckled and she smiled. "Isn't it?" he asked.

"No."

They rode on through the dark sagebrush and head-high junipers toward the low-roofed cabin and sun-bleached lodge-pole corrals. No sign of his horses in the pens. Tar Boy and Snake weren't here. The knowledge made him ride easier as some stock dogs came out barking to greet them.

A woman with prematurely gray hair came out and used her hand to shade her eyes. Recognizing Alma, she smiled and nodded to Dog.

"My lands, sister, what brings you over here?"

"Well, Sister Ruth, two men robbed Red of his money. Have you seen them?"

"A black and ah—Indian?"

'Yes." Alma dismounted.

"They and two women rode wide of this place yesterday."

Alma nodded and turned to Dog, who agreed. "Those were the robbers," she said.

"Get down and come in."

"No, thanks, we must go on. You don't have some good horses for sale, do you?"

"No, but Sister Sarah Carnes has some."

Alma looked at Dog—he nodded his approval.

"We'll see her about them." She hugged the woman and said something like bless you that Dog could barely hear.

They rode off and left Sister Ruth behind waving after them.

"What will she think?" he finally asked as they trotted westward at her directions.

"She will think I am escaping."

"But with a breed?"

"Indians are God's special children." She had to kick her horse hard to make him keep up so they could talk as they rode.

"Where is this next one at?" He rose and surveyed the country. Lots of dry bunchgrass between the sage—not a bad country for cows.

"Over at the base of that purple ridge. Too far out of our way?" She looked for his answer.

"No, we need better horses so I can find the trail. Will they be better horses?"

She nodded and didn't look over at him.

"What is wrong?" he demanded.

With a pull on the reins, she set her horse down and he did the same.

"There is something you aren't telling me?" he asked.

She held up her palm. "These horses may be stolen."

He began to laugh. Dropping his head, he stared at his own hands. She was worried he might not want them. Still amused, he booted the horse close to her and hugged her. "I have no fear of stolen horses if they are good ones."

"All right. You know."

It wasn't bad to have her. She knew these people well and she was smart. Besides, he could hardly wait to get in bed with her again. If they managed to get their hands on some good horses—they could run those thieves down in a few days.

They arrived at Sister Sarah Carnes's place at sundown. The older woman was straight-backed and acted displeased that Alma had even brought Red Dog. Finally relenting after Alma talked to her, she used a candle lamp to show them the horses in a corral.

Dog had no doubt the horses had been stolen when he first saw the five. There were two stout ranch horses out of them he liked, and he checked them close. They were sound enough as well as in good flesh.

"These," he said to Alma.

"Let me handle her."

He agreed. He'd have killed the old bitch and taken all five, but he didn't want Alma upset—yet. Besides, he liked this white woman—she would be valuable when he got the money. What was St. David like? He'd never been in a place it never snowed. It snowed in Denver and in Cheyenne. They were way south. What did he know, squatted in his moccasins, his back against the corral rails? The women talked in low voices over by the gate.

Soon Alma came and he stood up.

"We can have the horses," Alma said.

"She want yours?"

Alma nodded in the growing darkness. "I didn't think we needed them anyway."

"The gold ring?"

"Yes, that too and my milk cow."

"We're not—"

She pressed her finger to his lips. "She's going back for the cow herself. I think we should take the horses and leave."

"Yes." Damn, he wished he'd cut that gray-headed bitch's throat. Now he'd have to buy Alma a new gold ring. He caught the two, a blue roan and a chestnut gelding. They'd catch up with Tar Boy and Snake in two days on these horses. Satisfied, he tied them and went for the other two. He switched saddles and gear while she went off with Sarah. They were ready to ride, and he stole some packets full of corn and hung them on the saddle horns to feed the horses later.

Alma returned in the moonlight. "Why did you not come to the house?"

"I can tell she dislikes Indians."

"So," she said, and gave him some warm fresh bread with meat on it. "It would not have bothered you before."

"Before," he said between bites, "I would have killed her and taken all the horses."

She nodded that she understood and looked hard at the feed bags on her saddle before she mounted.

"She also gave us some feed," he said, and laughed. Wiping his mouth on the back of his hand, he shook his head. This woman of his had much to learn. That old biddy was no better than him—she sold stolen horses to desperate men. Was she better than a half-breed horse thief and stage robber? No.

They rode off and made a camp an hour later.

"When will we catch them?" she asked.

"In two days on these horses," he said, taking off the saddles as she spread out their blankets.

"Good. Without a fire, we better get under the covers."

"Yes," he said, feeling his dick grow hard for her.

They left camp in the predawn, and by noon had picked up the thieves' trail. The campfire ashes they found at noon were still warm from the night before. He nodded approval at her. They weren't far from the thieves. They'd need to be careful from there on. Snake could be like smoke too.

"Do you know this country?" he asked her.

"There is a store south of here. You can buy whiskey there."

"How far?"

She looked perplexed. "I'm not sure. I went there once in a wagon with Hiram to get supplies."

"No matter. They may be drunk there." He chuckled to himself. Like bait for a rat, Snake could never resist whiskey. No need to worry about how Dog would slip up on him—that breed bastard would be drunk if he ever got his hands on a bottle.

"What will we do?" she asked as they short-loped their horses.

"Get our money back."

She nodded with a grim look at him and sent her roan to running harder. Three hours later, they held up in sight of the smoke from the chimney streaking the sky. Their hard-breathing sweaty horses bobbed their heads, heated up from the long run.

He slipped off and handed her the reins. "Cool the horses," he said, and slid the Winchester out of the scabbard. "I'll slip up there and jump them."

"You need me?"

He shook his head. "I can handle them. I'll come for you when it's over."

"I could help—"

He put a finger on her lips and slowly shook his head. "I can handle this."

"Yes, but I will be worried about you." Her blue eyes looked pained.

He had never experienced such concern before over his well-being. The rifle raised over his head in a sign of defiance, he set out for the outpost in a jog. Using the broad junipers for cover, he zigzagged around the brushy evergreens until he could see the canvas-topped frame and false-front store. Stove smoke came from the rusty tin pipe stuck out of the back part of the structure's roof.

His horses were in a pen with packs on three of them. Maybe he had arrived in time. Crouched on his haunches, he tried to catch his breath and devise a plan to take the thieves. No doubt Snake and Tar Boy were inside the outpost—it was that backstabbing Mia he wondered about. He'd need to kill her first or she'd warn them.

No telling where she was at. Maybe he'd wait until dark and take them when they were drunk and asleep. He got a whiff of campfire smoke and smiled. He'd find that traitor Mia, kill her, then he'd take the other two.

He watched Mia, the fringe of her skirt whirling around her legs and arms as she busied herself making a meal at the campfire. There was no comparison between her body and that of the white woman. She had no breasts and did have a potbelly—besides, she never stirred when he fucked her. Never—endured him was all she did in bed.

Someone shouted, "Run Mia!" Then Dog's lights went out and he crashed facedown.

15

Slocum saw no smoke coming from the ranch house. A cow was bawling beside the corral. He stood in the stirrups for a better look around. Nothing. Were they too late? Had those three struck this place too?

Out of habit, he shifted the holster on his right side and then shot a hard glance at Lilly. "Be careful, they still may be around."

"The corral gate is open," she pointed out to him.

"I can see it is. They're still treacherous. Watch out for them."

Two sets of tracks from the corral went south. He dismounted to check and memorize them. A dozen brown hens ran over to join him as if he was a new source of feed.

"I'll check the house," she said, and swung her mule in that direction.

"Watch yourself," he said, and walked around the barnyard, looking for any clues. Why only two sets of tracks? Didn't make much sense. There were other prints, but they were older.

"No one's here," she shouted from the house.

Slocum studied the western sky. They were another day behind; the sun would soon set. "I'm coming after I unsaddle the mules."

"There's food and plenty of firewood here," she said loud enough to be heard.

"Good, I'm starved," he said, unlacing the latigos on One Ear. He pitched some hay for the mules, then went to the cabin with the bedroll on his shoulder.

Inside, he looked around in the flickering candlelight. "I'd say the person lived here left with them."

"Or was murdered. There are two sets of used dishes on the table."

"I guess we won't ever know unless they tell us. But this place was run by a woman, men aren't this neat."

"I'd agree, but there's no Bible here. There's several books that indicated they read." She nodded at the box shelves. "No Bible."

"Red Dog would never have stolen a Bible. Maybe they left to go see about someone or for supplies."

"I'm just relieved there is nobody here." She stood with her hands gloved in white flour at the dry sink and nodded as if relieved over the matter. "Even the sourdough starter is here."

He went over and hugged her shoulder. "Yes, that is good after all the rest we've been through. Bedding off the bed is gone too. Big mystery." He sighed deeply. "Tonight we have a roof over our heads anyway."

"There's a bathtub too."

"Good. I'll go draw some water from the well and we can heat it."

"Oh, that would be great," she said, looking pleased.

"No problem." He found two canvas buckets and began the process of packing the water in from the wooden-framed well cover, using the pulley to drop the tin pail and let it sink and hoist it up over and over again. The large iron kettle that swung in the hearth over the crackling fire soon heated the water while they ate fried salt pork slices, brown beans, and sourdough biscuits smeared with real butter and chokecherry jam.

His belly full, he leaned back in the chair. "Good food."

"I guess even out here they'd find you."

He nodded. "Someone would drop by and later he'd have a drink or two in some bar. Liquor would loosen his tongue. 'You'll never believe who I saw up in the Big Horns, my old captain from the war—Slocum.'"

He nodded and continued. "Some barkeep down the way polishing glasses would telegraph Fort Scott, Kansas, the next day for the reward, and a pair of deputies would be on their way."

She wiped her mouth on a towel. "I see. It's a total shame."

"That water should be getting warm," he said to change the subject. "I'll go take a long walk."

She wet her lips, shook her head, and looked hard at him. "We've shared beds. I thought tonight we'd share a bath."

"Your call." He studied her smooth face in the candlelight. All the restraint he'd had because of her loss drained away, and the release warmed him.

"I want it that way," she said.

He reached over and squeezed her hands. "So do I."

"I must sound very wanton."

"We aren't here to judge. Two people thrown into the wilderness. Who can we hurt?"

She looked relieved by his words. "You have a way, I am sure, with all the women, but I don't really care. Tonight we will have each other."

He nodded and finished his last biscuit coated in chokecherry jam, and considered what the sleek body he'd slept with would feel like under his hands and mouth. This would be a breathtaking night. For the moment, he hoped he had the restraint to hold out until she was ready.

The wooden bathtub was dragged out and filled half-full with steaming water, and then she began to undress. In the red-orange light, reflections of the colors shone on her bare skin as the clothes slipped away. Sitting on the chair, he toed off his boots, shed his shirt, all the time watching as she uncovered her full willowy figure. Then she stood naked, hugging her long breasts tipped by dark brown rosettes, ready to test the water with her toes. Satisfied, she stepped in and eased down in the tub.

With a wet cloth and bar of soap, she began to lather herself. He watched her movements. She had the grace of a ballerina onstage. The radiant fireplace was hot on his face, and his back, clad in his long-handle underwear, was cold as he stared at her efforts. No matter—this would be the night to share her body under the covers. Thoughts of her smooth skin pressed to his made him intoxicated with desire.

"We should have drawn straws for the first in the water."

"No," he said. "This way, I get to watch you and enjoy it."

"I have only one more bar of soap in my saddlebags and my supply will be depleted."

"Maybe we can find some."

She rinsed her arms off and rose, shedding water as he looked at her frontally for the first time. There were women in paintings and marble sculptures like her. His breath short, he tried to contain his urges.

"Better let me in there," he said, standing and undoing his one-piece underwear.

"I will," she said, and began to dry herself on the feed-sack towels.

"Then you need to get in under the covers. It must be getting real cold out here."

"I will—it is chilly."

He dipped out some more hot water, and hobbled over on his bare feet to add it to the tub. Then he slid in the water, and the warmth soaked quickly through his skin. He closed his eyes and when he opened them, she was kneeling beside him. He put an arm around her and they kissed. Her firm breast was in his chest as he savored her mouth.

"I didn't want you to forget our purpose," she said, and laughed softly.

"I ain't forgetting anything," he said, using the yellow bar of lye soap to lather his arms.

She tilted her head from side to side and rose. "I hope not."

His erection wasn't forgetting either, he decided. He quickly washed, rinsed, and took a dry towel from the nearby chair. She was in the bed with her face peering out and smiling. He'd see if he could widen that smile. Looking at the fireplace, he decided to toss some more wood on it before joining her. It would save getting up later.

Then he crossed the room and slid in under the covers she held up for his entry. The transfer from the chill in the room's air to the blankets and her body heat relaxed him as much as the bath. Their arms entangled, he sought her mouth and they locked lips. He pressed to her as one of her breasts crushed against him. Her silky legs parted and he dropped to his knees between them, taking some of his weight off her. He felt her palms slide over her belly and then down.

She eagerly directed his rising erection into her gates, and raised her butt off the bed for his entry. A soft cry escaped her lips when he pushed past her tight ring, and he began to pump his hard dick to her. She tossed her curly hair on the pillow and arched her back until their pubic bones rubbed against each other. Her clit grew hard and scratched the top of his blood-engorged tool forcing its way through her contracting walls.

Their breathing grew louder and their involvement hotter and deeper in the flames of passion's highest plateau. He was going wild in and out of her. Her fingers clutched his upper arms and she was moaning with pleasure.

Then he found the first wave of cum had left his testicles for her. Like two hot irons, one stuck in each side of his butt, the flames came bursting out the swollen head of his dick and filled her. She collapsed and hugged him hard.

"Oh, dear God—"

Raised up so his weight wasn't smothering her, he saw the tears that ran down her cheeks in the candlelight. He dropped his head down and kissed them away.

"Oh, Slocum—I never intended to cry."

"Hush. It's your right to cry."

She clutched him. "Stay in me. I still need you."

He agreed and savored their closeness. It was a nice night inside the cabin with a cold wind tearing at the eaves and three killers down the trail. Three men out there that needed to be brought to justice. His erection began to return as he moved it ever so slightly in and out of her.

A soft "Yes" escaped her lips.

16

Dog realized his sore head was in Alma's lap. What hit him? He had been creeping up on that traitor Mia and someone had knocked him out again.

"They left—" Alma said, and wet her lips.

"They get the rifle?" He blinked his eyes and tried to raise up.

"Stay down. You may have a concussion. There is a big knot on the back of your head."

They must have got the gun. "How long have they been gone?"

"A half hour or so. I was very worried they might have killed you."

He blinked his sore eyes up at her, realizing she had him covered by a blanket. No one had ever done all this for him.

"Our horses?"

"They're up in the cedars."

"Good. The rifle is gone?"

"Yes."

He looked at the azure sky and shook his sore head. "We can't go after them without a weapon. Damn it to hell."

"The Lord will provide," she said.

"The Lord—"

She put a finger on his lips to silence him. "He provided

you for me to escape that horrible ranch. He will provide you a weapon. Trust me."

"What? Rocks?"

"He will provide."

His head hurt too much to argue with her about religion. "You hear where they were going?"

"No, they rode south. I think they would have shot you, but several men over by the store were watching them. The black man shouted at the Indian not to shoot you and they rode out."

Twice he'd been saved. They were afraid of his spirit. How much of his money did they spend at this outpost? No telling—he needed a gun.

"There is food they left, if you can eat."

"I can eat." He looked up into her blue eyes.

"I will have to set your head down to get some." She looked worried about that.

"I'll be fine."

She took a folded blanket and put it under his head as she scooted out. On her feet, she ran to the fire and stoked it. He lay back and studied the sky. Needed a gun, needed to get after them, needed his head to stop pounding.

Who'd hit him this time? He didn't know. He heard Alma coming with food, and pushed himself up to a sitting position. Swinging the blanket around to his shoulders, he felt the fresh north wind. It would be cold by night.

"Here," she said, sitting down cross-legged before him with a bowl of stew. "I can feed you."

"I can feed myself," he grumbled, and nodded toward the things the thieves had abandoned by the campfire. "Did they leave anything we need?"

She handed him the bowl and spoon. "I'll go look."

He glanced up from the steaming stew to watch her search the things scattered around the fire. Bent over, she soon called out, "There is a gun and holster here."

He set down the bowl and swallowed a hot mouthful, which scorched his throat. It was his gun! She'd found his Colt among the things they'd left. He bounded to his feet, and then the world went black.

He heard her scream and he fell facedown.

"You all right?"

He looked up into her pale face and nodded. "I'll be fine."

"Lie still. I'll feed you. There's about ten new twenty-dollar gold pieces on the ground over there too. Must have spilled them."

"Good," he said, then smiled and lay back on her lap. His head hurt worse, but he felt better. Money and guns, those four wouldn't get far ahead of him and her. He'd run them in the ground and kill 'em with his bare hands.

The next morning he still felt too dizzy to ride, and they gathered up the things they could from what the thieves had left behind in their haste, and moved their camp to an empty shack hidden back in the junipers. She got the sheet-iron stove to working, and he felt warm for the first time in days. Propped up against the wall, he drank her willow-bark tea until the head pain let up. It really did work. She'd bought a deer haunch from the man at the store, and cooked Dog some venison in a stew of potatoes and dried green peas.

The food tasted good, but he still knew he was too light-headed to ride far. That gave the thieves another day's head start—maybe two if he didn't heal faster. He knew better than to ask her to go to the store and buy him some whiskey—Mormons hated whiskey, tea, and coffee.

He sat up and ate his supper, telling her how good the food tasted.

"There was a man and a woman at the store today. They were riding that bald-face horse and the dun Sarah Carnes had at her place."

He glared at her. "Who was he?"

"I don't know, but he wanted to know about Tar Boy and when he had left. The store man never mentioned us."

"You sure?"

"He's a Mormon. He'd never tell him a thing about us."

"You sure?"

"Yes." She looked down hard at his hand gripping her forearm.

He released her. "Yeah, yeah. Was this man law?"

"Tall man. Dark beard and hair—"

"Tom White—the sumbitch. Who was the woman?"

'I don't know, but they were together—you can tell when a man and woman are together."

"What did they do?"

"Rode off to Atlantic City, I guess. Looking for Tar Boy. They'd been to my place too and mentioned it was empty. Brother Yates never said a word—shook his head like he didn't know anything about it."

"Good, we can let him get Snake and Tar Boy and we get *him*."

"You better not get too worked up. When you're better, we can go after them if you have to."

Have to? He had to because they had his money. What they hadn't spent, dropped on the ground, or wasted, they had on them. In the morning he'd be strong enough to ride. Had to be.

17

Atlantic City was a treeless cluster of false-front buildings, shacks, and tents in a sagebrush sea. It had existed on the emigration trail for all the years that wagon trains rolled westward. Most new settlers by this time used the various cross-country railroads to come West, and the town, which was miles from the tracks, had begun to fall into a depression as fewer and fewer wagons rumbled past its gates.

A minor gold rush had quickly petered out, and it became more of a hangout for wanted men, horse thieves, outcast whores with no future, and the typical riffraff hiding from some dark secret past, hoping not to be known.

Slocum set the bald-face horse down and studied the smoke columns from various rusty stovepipes poking through roofs. He glanced over at Lilly with regret that she wasn't back in Texas where the sun had some heat and there weren't any threats to her like those that might lie ahead.

"You look concerned," she said, and shivered in the sharp air.

"Atlantic City is a tough place. For your own safety I wish you weren't here." He paused, feeling pained for her welfare.

"I can shoot. I can fight."

He rubbed his left palm on top of his pants leg. "This

132

place is a hellhole. Those killers might be choirboys in this town's crowd."

"Slocum, I'm here and I can fight. Let's get on with it."

"One thing. Shoot first and ask questions later."

She nodded.

Against his gut feeling, he booted the bald-face horse off the ridge. Mrs. Carnes had said the tracks he'd followed to her front door were those of a Mormon husband and wife. Slocum still doubted it. After swapping horses with Carnes, he'd lost their tracks heading back to the store.

He felt certain the two horses they rode had been stolen, probably in Utah. What business did a "Morman widow" have with that kind of high-priced horseflesh on a two-bit ranch in the brakes? But he carried two bills of sales that were supposed to be authentic for their mounts—so as long as the real owner didn't recognize them, they'd be fine. He had to agree with Lilly that it beat the fire out of riding those iron-jawed mules.

Following the wagon tracks that straddled a dry short-grass ribbon between them, they soon reached the main street. He wished he knew what those killers were riding. But the nondescript horses standing windblown and hipshot at various racks offered him little information.

He indicated the livery and she agreed, looking steely-eyed at the weather-beaten structures and few residents out in the cold. A grizzly face or two on the boardwalk took her in, and then spit tobacco into the street like a period at the end of the sentence when she passed them.

They dismounted, and she held the reins while he struggled against the wind to open the big faded red door. A hostler soon came and assisted him, indicating that she should hurry and bring the two horses inside. With the door closed, the livery, smelling of horse piss, was dark save for some light coming through the gaps in the siding.

"Ten cents a day—twenty-five with grain."

"Grain them after you water 'em and they cool down." Slocum looked around. "Is there a place we can stay without bedbugs?"

The old man leaned over, squeezed his nose, and sent out a stream of phlegm. He wiped his fingers on the side of his britches and nodded. "There's an empty shack on the hill out back. Been empty for months. Got a good stove, some coal, and firewood."

"Why ain't someone used it?"

He smiled in the half-light from under his gray beard. "'Cause I got it locked."

"Yours?"

"Yeah, I stay down here. Cost you two bits a day."

"Here's two dollars. We'll see how long we're going to stay."

"Good enough. Tie them horses, I'll put them up," the old man said to Lilly. "I'll show you out the back door to the place."

"Good," Slocum said. "Has there been a black man and breed in town?"

"Buffalo soldier?"

"No, he's civilian."

The old man rubbed his hand over his bearded mouth. "I seen a couple blacks, but I thought that they was deserters."

"His name's Tar Boy and he's running with a Sioux breed called Snake. There is another one called Red Dog, Sioux breed."

"You looking fur them?"

Busy taking their bedroll off the saddle, Slocum turned to him and said, "Yes. They murdered her husband."

He swept off his shapeless felt hat. "Sorry, ma'am."

"Thank you," she said with her arms loaded. "Show us the way."

The force of the wind tore the walk-through back door from the old man's grasp. He swore, then caught his hat with one hand. "Better give you the key." He took it from around his neck on a leather cord and gave it to her with an extra pat on the top of her hand.

"Need anything, holler."

"We will, "Slocum promised, and she thanked him.

Two trips and they had their things inside the snug shack

and a fire going. Except for some sheet metal that rattled on the roof, the place suited both of them. She brewed some coffee on the cookstove and made him a list of things she wanted from the store, including cinnamon and sugar to make rolls.

It was the first time since they found the abandoned ranch house that they'd been under a roof together. He settled back on their bedroll atop the rope bed in the room's growing warmth and listened to the wind as well as to her singing "Sweet Betsy from Pike."

"First time you've sung. Sounds good."

Looking embarrassed, she nodded. "I guess it was the first time I wanted to sing."

"Hey, I know it hasn't been a Sunday-school picnic for you."

"No," she said, and sat down on the edge of the bed. "Without me along you'd probably already have caught them."

"I doubt that." He studied the highlights in her curly hair from the shaft of light coming in the small four-pane window.

Pursing her lips, she bent over him. "I know I've held you back."

He swept her up in his arms and drew her down on top of him. "It's been a helluva nice trip."

Then he kissed her, and they were soon lost to it all.

Dark came early in the short day. After they ate supper, he cleaned his .44 Colt, re-oiled it, and loaded it with five cartridges. He spun the cylinder till the hammer rested on an empty. Then he holstered it. Time to go look for them. Rats came out at night.

She came over and kissed him. She'd finished washing their dishes and drying the last of them. "You be careful tonight."

"Careful as I can be. You keep that door barred till I get back, and shoot first, ask questions later."

"Yes, sir."

He put on his jumper and felt hat, dreading the night wind. She walked him across the small shack to the door. He kissed her good-bye with his mind full of regret about not staying there, and then went into the starry night. The bitter north wind pushing him, he strode down the hillside on the wagon tracks between the dark clumps of sagebrush toward the outline of buildings. A few lights showed in windows. He could hear some music as he approached the town from the back side and went between two buildings to mount the sidewalk. Standing for a moment to let his eyes adjust to the darkness, he observed two drunks hanging on to each other and slurring their words as they wandered past and never noticed him. The saddle and harness shop was dark. Next he came to a saloon. The sounds from inside of a piano playing and some singing reached out into the night. In the starlight, he could read the name on the swinging sign: S.S. CANARY. Strange name for a saloon in the Wyoming sagebrush sea.

He tried the thumb latch and the door caught on the threshold and scraped open. In the smoky interior, a leggy woman seated in a man's lap, about to spill out of the top of her red dress, shouted, "Howdy, partner."

He nodded to acknowledge her greeting. A piano player was tinkling the ivories to a snappy tune. Some fat woman in an equally low-cut dress was warbling the words to it. He felt several sharp eyes assessing him as he walked to the bar and ordered a beer. Hard to tell much for all the haze in the room—lots of shouting and women shrieking.

"Here's your beer. Be ten cents, laddie," the bartender said, and set down the glass with foam overflowing the rim.

He paid the man, then turned to look over the mob. No familiar hats were in sight. Snake wore an unblocked black hat with a trailing eagle feather, Tar Boy a Boss of the Plains Stetson, and Red Dog a battered hat with curled brim sides.

When the short red-faced bartender wasn't busy, Slocum called him over.

"Whatcha need? Some pussy?"

"Not tonight." He lowered his voice and put a silver dollar on the bar. With two fingers on top of it, he indicated the coin could belong to the man. Probably a day's wages for him, or more.

"A black man been in here lately?" Slocum asked.

The man frowned as if thinking hard. Blacks were not that common in the West, except for the buffalo soldiers, and none were stationed close around Atlantic City. The man leaned forward and in a soft whisper said, "A black and a breed with two squaws rode into town yesterday or the day before—I thought it was a strange outfit when I seed it."

Slocum nodded. Easter might be one of them. He hated that notion. "You know where they went?"

"No, but there's a camp of blanket-ass Injuns and white trash west of here at Oatman Springs. More than likely, that's where they'd land."

"How far is it?"

"Three, four miles. Follow the wagon tracks, you can't miss it. Shacks and lodges."

Slocum slid the coin over. "Thanks."

"Any time, laddie." He quickly pocketed his reward.

Slocum finished his beer, and had started to go when one of the women tried to lure him into her bed. Inebriated, she stumbled into him on her high heels, spilling some champagne on his jumper.

"Oh, sorry—" she slurred, and used her hand to try and wipe away the liquid.

"No problem, ma'am."

She laughed out loud at his words. "Oh, you're so nice." Then, in a clumsy fashion, she snuggled against him, and he took her by the arms so she didn't fall.

With a toss of her brittle-looking hair, she flashed a smile. "I'm the best fuck in Atlantic City, cow—boy."

He set her against the bar for support, and touched his hat brim to show her that he was leaving. "I don't doubt that. Right now I am busy. Excuse me."

"Go on, you son of a bitch," she shouted after him. "Go screw your horse or some damn sheep!"

Her words drew a roar of laughter and comments. Slocum

ignored them and rebuttoned his jumper against the night before he ducked outside. On the porch, he let his eyes adjust to the darkness. There was some light spilling out the front windows.

If Tar Boy and Snake were at Oatman Springs, where was Red Dog? Perhaps he was there already. Slocum would sure have to cover his backside. Snake didn't get his handle from his righteous ways. The other two were not Sunday-school students either. By themselves or apart, they all could be deadly.

He hiked up the hill listening to the sounds of the town dwindle. Maybe come daylight, he'd find them and end this business.

"It's me," he shouted at the shack's door. "Don't shoot."

"Silly," she said, and undid the bar to let him inside.

"Well, what did you learn?" she said as he took off his coat in the warm interior.

"They're here or have been. I'll find out in the morning."

"Where are they?"

"A camp west of here."

"I'm going."

He took her in his arms and hugged her. "We'll see."

"I'm going with you."

He looked up at the ceiling. He'd see about that.

18

Red Dog met an old Indian and his squaw on the road. The buck rode the horse that pulled the travois. His woman walked behind and carried a heavy pack.

"Ho," he said to the man as he and Alma reined up.

"I am looking for a white man and woman. One rides a bald-faced horse." He looked over, and Alma nodded that he was right about the horse.

The leather-faced old man nodded and then asked. "You got 'bacco?"

Dog shook his head. The old devil wanted payment for his answer. He'd probably done that all his life to white men—he didn't think Dog was any more than that—a white man's spawn.

Flush with anger, Dog pushed his horse in close to him and in Sioux said through his teeth, "If you wish to piss out your dick anymore, tell me about them and be quick, or I'll cut it off right here."

The old one's brown eyes opened wide in shock. He held up his right palm to attest to what he spoke. "We see them riding south. Big man. Tall white woman."

Dog nodded, and turned his horse away and spoke to Alma. "He knows nothing. Let's go. They are still ahead of us."

She moved out to join him. "Do you know him?"

He shook his head. "Some old Sioux that married that Shoshone woman."

"I feel sorry for her." She glanced back at the pair, already started out for the north.

"It is the Indian way."

"That's not any better than the *Mormon way*."

"I won't treat you like that."

"Good."

"Do you regret leaving that place with me?"

"Oh, no." She smiled. "I just don't want to have to ever go back."

"Good." He booted his horse into a trot. She could count the money for him. Be nice to know how much he had when he got it all back from those two. "Come on. We must be near Atlantic City. We will make camp soon and you can go in town and learn what you can."

They camped on a dry creek. He found water by digging out the sand and letting it seep into the pit. Meanwhile, she gathered firewood under the gnarled cottonwoods and soon had a smoky fire going. The horses drank from the pit, and then he fed them the last of the grain in nose feeders. Then he tied their leads to a tree and brought her a canvas pail of water for cooking.

He warmed his hands at the fire and nodded his approval. "We should find those thieves tomorrow."

She nodded, putting the kettle of dry beans and water over the fire. "Could we just go on and forget them?"

"No."

"I didn't suppose so."

"They have all my money. My head is still sore from them beating on it."

"It says in the Bible that revenge is mine saith the Lord."

"It ain't his money either that they stole." He forced down his anger at her.

She nodded and huddled under a blanket while seated on the ground. "I don't want you hurt."

"I won't get hurt."

"You will if you mess with them again. They would have shot you if there had not been those men watching it happen. I don't know what I would do without you. I've never been in this place before. I turned my back on *them* when I left up there."

He moved beside her and hugged her. "I will care for you."

She nodded to show she'd heard him, but never raised her chin.

"In the blankets tonight I'll make you forget your worries," he said.

With a forced smile for him, she agreed. "I need that. Thank you."

He tossed a handful of twigs on the fire. The dry cottonwood sticks made a smoky blaze. The beans would be a while.

"The beans can cook," he said, and motioned to the bedroll.

She needed no second urging. She rose and hurried over, taking off her moccasins and shedding her skirt, then ducking under the blankets. He removed his footgear and took down his galluses, unbuttoning his fly. Under the cold blankets, they quickly were in each other's arms. He fit between her knees, and his rising probe touched her smooth warm legs on its route to her source. The lubrication felt cool, but the head of his dick was soon buried in her warm oven and he was pumping into her.

She pulled the covers over his shoulders and shut out the chill. In the starlight, he could see her eyes dissolve into pleasure's glassy glare. He was going after her hard and her walls responded by contracting. When she began to softly moan in the arms of passion, he grew even more excited. Then he knew that he would soon explode and thrust himself to the depth of her well, and fired point-blank against it.

A soft cry came from her throat as she threw her head back and gasped aloud. "Oh. God—"

They lay for a long while coupled—savoring the time silently. At last she asked to check on her cooking and he let her go. She rushed back and snuggled against him. The cold skin of her legs pressed to his warm surface.

"It will be a while," she said, out of breath.

"Good," he said, and climbed over on top of her. "I have more."

Dawn came in an icy silence. Dog ate some beans still warm in the kettle over the ashes. A thick frost was on everything. Handing her the empty bowl, he told her to stay warm, he'd be back. He saddled his horse, huffing great clouds of breath as he worked. In the saddle, he waved to her and rode off to the south. When he had that money back, they could go to St. David and live in a big house and have lots of help.

With her, he could have respect. He made his horse trot. The sooner this was over, the sooner he could leave this cold place. His resolve to have them all in his gun sights was strong. They'd know better than to mess with him when they went to hell. Before he was done, he'd kill Tom White too.

In town, he found an old drunk Indian in the alley. He questioned him in sign language, and the old man was not very clear. Talked about some springs west of there. They were there. The black man and the breed with an eagle feather on his new hat and two squaws. Dog paid him two bits.

He went back to his horse, mounted him, and rode around the town to get on the road. By mid-morning, he could see the camp from where he lay on his belly. Smoke from cooking fires settled around the lodges, and he noticed something else. The red piebald horse from that bitch's corral was hobbled in a draw. *Tom White*.

He drew back. His skin felt clammy despite the cold. Where was White? He must be watching the camp too. Or was he watching *him*? Dog slowly moved backward. Let White kill them and then he'd kill White. He looked carefully right and left. No sign of White, but Dog didn't want him to know that he wasn't in the camp with the others. He kept to his belly until he slipped in to the wash, and then, bent low, he ran for his horse.

He'd go back to the town, buy some whiskey, and then return to Alma and his own camp later. He deserved a drink. Tom White—that sumbitch needed killing too. He would catch him unaware. That white man was no ghost, he'd get him. Dog's hands were shaking as he rode east in the cold wind. The low sun was no help. Shivering under the blanket on his shoulders, he wondered how he'd ever learn if White had killed them.

He'd have the old Injun buy him some whiskey. Back at Atlantic City, he found him in the same alley.

"Go buy two pints of good whiskey," he said, giving the old man four dollars in silver. That should be enough even for an Indian to buy that much whiskey.

The old man agreed and got up stiffly. Huddled under the blanket, Dog noticed the rider and the sorrel bald-face horse coming back to town. He wrapped himself deeper so White would not recognize him. Then Dog watched him put his horse in the livery, and moments later go out the front and hurry away.

His fingers itched for the pistol in the holster on his hip. Had White shot the others? Dog bet he hadn't. He wouldn't have came back to town so fast. Good thing Dog saw that horse—White and his woman could wait, he'd get all of them.

The whiskey was better than most he'd had to drink in his life. Sitting on their butts in the sunshine, he and the old drunk shared the alley space side by side. The liquor even warmed Dog's cold ears as he sipped it. With a nod of approval to his partner, he soon finished it feeling mellow.

A deep rusty voice said, "You gawdamn Injuns are drunk again, huh?"

Dog realized he'd soon be in jail. Alma would be alone out there. She'd think he'd abandoned her. He needed to do something.

"Guess a couple days in the pokey are what you need." The red-faced man wearing the silver badge looked huge as he bent over to pull them both up by their collars.

He wasn't ready for the muzzle of the .45 that Dog drove

into his big gut. The lawman straightened and released them. His blue eyes opened wide and the shocked look paled his ruddy complexion. "Put-put that gun away—"

The .45 spoke in Dog's hand, and the deputy grabbed for his belly. Shot number two took him in the face. He staggered back and then slumped to his knees, and fell facedown at Dog's feet. Good enough for him.

"Oh, sweet Jesus!" the old Indian said, wrapping his filthy blanket tightly around him. "Big trouble now."

"For you maybe. I'm leaving." He holstered his gun, then balled up his blanket, and headed for the far end of the alley in a run. Ignoring the shouts after him to come back, he ducked to the left at the back of the livery, then ran down the wash and mounted his horse.

He was racing hard for his camp. Looking back for pursuit. He needed to get Alma and be gone. Shooting a lawman was bad business. When he topped the ridge, he saw no smoke.

Where was that woman? Why no fire? Why no sign of the other horse? Had she left him?

He slid the horse to a stop and bolted off the saddle. She was on the ground facedown—not moving. She'd been scalped. No—no—no. He turned her stiff body over and saw her knife-mutilated breasts and the large stick jammed into her privates. Only one man could do such a vile act.

He screamed at the sky, "Snake, I will find you and eat your liver!"

Then, realizing there might be a posse coming after him any minute, he rummaged for a few things to eat—crackers, dry cheese, some candy. With shaking hands, he put them in his saddlebags. Snake had stolen her horse too. Damn. He needed to be gone. The next place where they could hide was Green River. He'd have to find them there.

Tears streaked his face. His jaw trembled. Snake must have come right after he left, or had been waiting for him to leave. Shame that worthless breed didn't die up there with Yellow Hair.

Dog started to mount, but stopped and staggered around as he retched. The vile fumes filled his nose and triggered more reactions as he bent over puking and then having dry heaves that gagged him. Finally, weak and depleted, he rode out of camp, his vision blurred by the wetness.

Alma.

19

"There's a man on horseback coming up here," Lilly said, standing at the window and turning back toward him.

Slocum rose and buckled on his gun belt. "Wonder what he wants."

He put on his jumper and hat and she unbarred the door. He stood on the weathered gray boards that made a mud stoop to greet the man.

"Howdy. Can I help you?"

"Withers my name." The clean-shaven man in his thirties sat his bay horse in the slump of no stranger to the saddle. "A deputy sheriff was shot about twenty minutes ago by a breed in the alley. Old Sam said you were asking about one."

Slocum nodded. "What did he look like?"

"Can't tell you. No one seen him but an old drunk Injun, and he's pretty drunk."

"What can I do?"

"Thought you might throw in with us. We're going after him. Charlie—the deputy—had a wife and some kids."

Slocum considered a moment. Tar Boy and two women with a pack string had left the springs at dawn headed west. No one seemed to know where Snake went—they'd not seen him since the day before. Nor had anyone up there seen anyone answering Dog's description. This breed who shot the deputy could be either of them.

"I'll get my rifle. My horse—"

"I'll go get him at the livery, be right back." Withers turned and rode off in a lope.

"Who do you think it is?" Lilly asked.

Slocum shrugged. "Might be either of them. Or none. But for a drunk breed to shoot a deputy makes me think it could be either of them."

With a proud grin, she straightened his jumper collar. "Just be sure to come back for me."

"I promise."

She hugged him and rested her forehead on his. "Good."

"I have no idea how long we'll be gone."

"I'll be fine."

"Shoot first."

"I will." She turned at the sound of a horse returning. "Didn't take him long."

He winked, kissed her, and went outside with his rifle.

"Never caught your name," Withers said, holding out the reins to Baldy. "Call me Joe."

"Tom, Tom White," Slocum said, and waved to her from the saddle.

"That your wife?" Joe asked, looking impressed.

"These breeds I am looking for killed her husband up in the Big Horns. She wanted to come along. It was that or take three days getting her back to civilization."

"Nice job," Joe said, and they sent their horses into a lope. "Posse has a lead on us. I thought you might help."

"Glad to." They rode on hard until the five riders ahead came in sight and they joined them.

"Sheriff," Joe said to the taller man riding stirrup to stirrup in a hard trot. "Tom White. He thinks he knows the killer. He was looking for him too."

"Glad you came, White. His tracks are easy to follow right now, but a breed can sure hide them if he tries. Where you reckon he's headed?"

"No idea, Sheriff."

"Still glad to have you all the same." He nodded, drew down the brim of his hat, and faced the fresh wind.

"There's a camp up there!" Someone pointed.

They rode up, and several turned away at the sight of the woman's mutilated body.

"Scalped too," someone said, and forced himself not to puke.

"Know her, Tom?" the sheriff asked.

"No." Slocum studied the ground and dropped down to look hard at the tracks. "I saw these same footprints at a deserted, small ranch about four days ago in the south end of the Big Horns."

"Reckon they kidnapped her?"

"I have no idea. Mrs. McCullem and I found a deserted ranch. We never could find out any more about who lived there or why they'd left. But I'd bet one thing. This was done by a breed called Snake. There's two pairs of footprints of men's moccasins. One made by someone who was here a lot, the other on top of the first."

"Who's Snake?" the sheriff asked.

"He did some scouting for the army. Word is he tried to sign on with Custer. Him being half Sioux, the Crow scouts said no."

"Might get a description out of the Army of the West in Omaha." The sheriff rose stiffly. "Need someone to take the body back to town."

A boy of perhaps seventeen stepped up. "I'll do that, sir."

"Jordan, I don't mean to put such a job on you, but take her to the undertaker. He'll do the rest."

The others rounded up some of the dirty blankets and wrapped her for him. Then when the boy was mounted, they eased her body over his lap and sent him on with his cargo.

Slocum felt certain about the two sets of tracks. One was from the man the posse followed. The other set was from the second man on the scene, who'd obviously secured his horse in a draw a short distance away. That one had led a horse down to his own and ridden out. Both men had left the site of her murder and gone southwesterly.

"How far ahead are they?" the sheriff asked. "We only have a few more hours of daylight."

"No telling," Slocum said.

"Let's ride, maybe we can catch them."

Everyone else agreed and they pressed on. The sharp wind cutting his face, Slocum pulled up his kerchief as they dropped off along a slope that turned to the south. Sagebrush brushed his boot toes, but the two sets of tracks were clear enough that they could follow them—maybe to hell and gone. He had no way to know.

As the day dragged on, Slocum felt certain both men were headed for the emigrant road—perhaps to catch up with Tar Boy. Slocum had been told that Tar Boy had left Oatman Springs, going to the west with two Indian women. Easter was no doubt one of those women. The notion niggled him, but he had no way to aid her. This horrific murder and mutilation of the white woman had upset him. How did she fit into the scheme of things? The answers weren't spilling out for him. Why kill a woman like that?

He reined Baldy around some junipers, and looked far to the south for any sign of dust or the two men. Nothing but the distant snowy peaks in Colorado. More than likely, they planned to hole up around the Green River—it was several days' ride south and west.

Which one of them shot the deputy? And what were they doing in Atlantic City anyway? Lilly. The notion struck him. Would she be their next victum? Damn. Had he gone off and left her exposed to the same ruthless killer?

He pushed Baldy up beside the sheriff. "How much farther is the emigrant road?"

"I guess five to ten miles. Why?"

"I'm concerned this madman may double back to harm Mrs. McCullem."

"Why's that?" The lawman frowned.

"These breeds we're tracking and a black man that recently

rode out of Oatman Springs are responsible for her husband's murder up in the Big Horns. They're a gang of robbers that drifted down from Montana."

The sheriff shook his head in disapproval. "Pretty tough bunch. I don't blame you for having concern. That was the worst murder back there I ever saw in my life."

"It was. If I cut southeast, I figure I can reach Atlantic City or at least the emigrant road."

"You should—it'll take several hours, but that would be the best way. Go ahead. We ain't prepared for much more either. I'd hoped they'd stop and make camp, but I'm beginning to believe they won't. Since you seem to know about them, what's your take on it?"

"You've seen their handiwork. When we found them, her husband and his foreman looked as bad as that woman did."

"They need to be stopped before they do anything else."

Slocum agreed. "I'm headed to see about her."

"I understand. Thanks for your help. We may be tracking ghosts."

"No, they're not ghosts." Slocum gave him a wave and used a game trail that forked off to the left.

He pushed Baldy hard. A large stone filled his empty stomach as the shadows grew longer and he knew daylight would soon leave him. A red sundown blazed the wide sky and sunk into twilight. The country was fairly level to tilted, and Baldy acted like he had good sense as Slocum kept him in a long trot. In the distance, a wolf howled and another answered.

In a short while, he spooked some range horses that thundered away like he was after them. Then some grazing mule deer threw their heads up and bounced away on steel springs into the pearly starlight.

Night wore on, until finally he saw the blinking lights in the distance. Atlantic City. He gave Baldy his head when they struck some wagon tracks. At the cabin door, he reined up the hard-breathing horse and knocked on the door.

"Lilly? Lilly?"

"Yes—"

He sagged against the wall at the sound of her voice.

"I'm coming," she said.

His strength depleted, he waited and glanced around in the moonlight, wondering where those killers were at.

"Did you find the killers?" she asked as she opened the door.

"No. All we found was a murdered white woman. I've—" He let out a sigh, hugged and kissed her. "I was so worried they might come back here and hurt you."

"I'm fine. What will you do with Baldy?" She motioned to the horse.

"Take him to the livery and be back."

'Wait, I'll go along." She went back inside to finish dressing.

In a few minutes, she joined him outside and they started for the livery. "Who was she?"

"They may never know. I have thought and thought about it. They may have split up and she may have been with one of them."

"Why would a white woman have joined them?"

Leading Baldy as they walked downhill, he slapped the reins against his leg. "Damned if I know. Those people up in the mountains told us little about anything. Guarded as they acted, we never knew more than the tracks we followed."

"I don't guess you knew her?"

"No, I'd never seen her before." A wave of revulsion shook his shoulders as he recalled her fate.

"What will we do next?"

"I think I better go check the Green River country."

"I'll go too."

"Lilly, go back to Texas. That mess up there today was so bad."

"Remember, it was my husband and his foreman they killed."

"But capturing them—"

She blocked his path and he about walked into her. "I'm going. Besides, I have to admit I like your company. I don't know if I'd have made it without you."

They hugged each other tight until he noticed her sniffle and released her. "You okay?"

She wiped her nose on a handkerchief. "I'm fine. Let's get him put up. It's cold out here."

They walked on toward the dark shape of the livery.

"You know, one day I'll have to move on."

She nodded beside him. "Just not yet."

No—not yet.

20

Dog sat his horse and looked across the sprawling Red Desert before him. Nothing for miles but gray-black sagebrush. He'd taken a meal and spent a night with a stinking sheepherder sleeping in his wagon. He still remembered the old man's food tasting of wool. The herder had not seen Snake, though he had crossed close to him sometime earlier. Dog had seen his tracks.

He'd lost Snake's trail a couple of times—but he'd not wasted much time finding it again. The tracks of the horse that Snake rode were easy to see. But there'd been no sight of him, and Dog had expected to catch him by this time. He would make that worthless breed pay for killing Alma.

He spotted a sun-browned canvas cover on a wagon. Might be some lost settlers. He approached it with care, sizing up whether they'd be worth robbing. Most were penniless and without food. He saw smoke from a cooking fire swirling low on the ground.

Maybe he could get a meal—the wool taste was still in his mouth. Made him want to gag. He urged his horse down the slope toward the wagon.

A woman raised up from her cooking and swept the loose lock of black hair back from her face as he rode up. A white woman in her twenties, small eyes, sharp nose, not pretty, and thin like a buggy whip.

"Hello," she said.

"Howdy. You got any food I can buy?" He waited in the saddle for her reply.

"Some antee-lope stew." She never blinked or took her gaze off him.

"I can pay you."

She shook her head. "Never costed me much. Man gave us that antee-lope."

"I would appreciate it. Your man here?"

"Gone to get a wheel fixed. He'll be along shortly."

Then he noticed the four oxen grazing in the draw and nodded. He stepped down and dropped the reins. His horse snorted in the dust and went to grazing on the dry bunchgrass.

"I'm looking for another breed, he rode by here."

She nodded. "Earlier, never stopped. I saw his hat and feather, and when I saw you, I figured he'd came back."

Dog shook his head and squatted down across the fire from her. "You were lucky he rode by. He's a killer and a bad one. Murdered my wife."

'Oh, I'm sorry." She dished him out some stew on a plate and handed it over.

Dog had his own spoon, and nodded to her before he tried the first spoonful. It was so hot it burned his mouth and made his eyes water. "Good," he managed to say in approval of the food.

"Where's he going?" she asked.

"To hell when I catch him." He looked down at the stringy meat on his spoon and shook his head over Snake passing so close. Why had he done that? Had to be a good reason. Wonder he'd never raped and kilt this woman. "You are very lucky."

"I'm sure glad you warned me."

Then it clicked in his head like a revolver cylinder locking in place. She was part of Snake's plan unbeknownst to her. Snake rode by first so she could see him, then figured that Dog would come next, find her alone, and rape her. While he raped her, Snake would creep back, get to kill him, and take her.

Good plan, but Dog would disappoint him. Snake must be

out in that sage on his belly creeping up on the wagon. No need to look for him—Dog would lay a trap. With a small smile in the corner of his mouth, he shoveled in more stew.

"Where's he going? I mean, like, the town?" she asked.

"No telling." He handed her back the plate.

"More?"

"No—it was good."

She nodded.

"We're being watched," he said softly, feeling Snake's presence close by.

Her blue eyes flew wide open. "What—by-by who?"

His eyes in a half-squint, he searched the rolling purple-tinted sage. "Start for the back of the wagon and don't you look around. It might warn him."

"You mean that killer?" Her face paled.

"Act like I am dragging you there." He took hold of her arm.

"Why?"

He tightened his grip on her. "So he thinks I am distracted by you. And go to shouting 'no.' "

She swallowed hard and then sensing he was earnest, she nodded. "No! No!"

"Kick and try to hit me."

She began to have a fit as he hurried her on. "Good," he whispered. "Louder. Our lives depend on this."

"Oh, no! Stop!"

He shoved her ahead up the steps and into the wagon. Once inside, he drew his Colt and told her to scream and wail. Squatted on the floor inside the oval opening, he waited, his breath rushing through his nose.

"Now protest softer."

She sat, hugging her arms and shaking. As she was huddled and drawn in a ball against crates and sacks of flour and beans, the tears streamed down her face.

Pistol cocked, he waited, reaching over with his free hand to grip the side board and make the wagon rock from time to time like he and the woman were struggling. Then, out of nowhere, the unblocked hat and dark chiseled face appeared in the opening before him. Snake's diamond eyes widened in shocked disbelief seconds before Dog's Colt blasted him in the face and the acrid gun smoke boiled up in the wagon's confines.

With a scream, Dog charged out onto the steps and emptied the rest of his bullets in Snake's body at point-blank range. The big knife spilled out of Snake's hand. With fumbling fingers, Dog tried to unload and reload his Colt. Where was Tar Boy?

Copper cartridges spilled on the ground. At last, the job completed, eaten up with his own anxiety, he stood weak-kneed and hatless over the still body. Every bad word he knew flowed silently at the dying ex-scout whose legs jerked in death's arms.

On her hands and knees at the back of the wagon, tears streaming down her face, the woman whined, "How did you ever know he was out there?"

Dog shook his head and swallowed—he just knew.

He went and found Snake's white horse hidden in a dry wash. All the time he kept searching around, fearful that the black might be lurking out there too. No other tracks but Snake's. Where was that black sumbitch at?

Wary enough and riding the white horse, he hurried back to the wagon.

He dismounted and hitched the horse beside his own. No need in wasting Snake's clothes and boots. Snake would damn sure not need them again.

"Get over here and help me get him undressed," he said.

The woman stood back, chewing on her knuckles, and stared horrified as he twisted off Snake's moccasins. Hell with her. He undid the man's pants and gun belt, then jerked his britches off and the jumper shirt, and at last stripped off his long handles. Lying on his back, naked as a jay, his scrotum all shriveled and donkey-dick limb, Snake looked harmless enough.

With her back to the corpse, she gasped and clung to the tall wagon rim. "Oh, you're horrible, treating the dead like that."

"Lady, you look at him and look hard. 'Cause he'd've had that dick of his up you, and then he'd've cut your throat like he did my woman. He stuck a stick bigger than my fist in her pussy before she died."

"Oh," she wailed, and clasped her hands together. "Dear Father God—"

With a disapproving shake of his head over her wailing, he took a lariat off Snake's saddle and tied it around his bare feet. Then Dog climbed on his pony, dallied the rope on the horn, and rode off in the sagebrush dragging him out of camp so she didn't have to look at his ugly brown body till her man came home.

When Dog came back and dismounted, she asked him in a soft voice, "Ain't yeah even going to bury him?"

"He never buried my woman."

She nodded, but still looked taken aback by his manner.

He indicated the back of the wagon. "I guess you better get back in that wagon and get undressed."

She frowned at him.

"I better finish what we started."

"You—you won't hurt me?"

"Not if you hurry and get undressed and on your back in them blankets." He pointed her toward the set of steps.

She nodded in surrender, skirt in hand, and headed for the wagon. Halfway, she stopped. "What if you don't like me?"

"Oh, I'll like it fine. Hurry."

"I am. I am."

Afterward, he mounted his horse, and with Snake's pony on a lead rope, he started to leave. She stood in the back of the wagon holding a blanket over her nakedness, and watched him with a blank look on her face.

She sure was the skinniest woman he'd even crawled on top of. Now he needed to find Tar Boy and the money. With a shake of his head, he booted his horse southwestward.

21

Slocum tossed their saddles and pads on the Pullman car's platform, then their war bags and bedrolls. The porter was busy dragging them in the door, smiling each time he reappeared for another load. Then Slocum helped Lilly up the stairs, and they left Rawlins for Rock Springs as the conductor shouted, "All aboard."

"Tell me about this Green River country," Lilly said as the sagebrush desert flew by the smudged window at twenty-five miles per hour.

"It's like that broken desert country around where we found the abandoned ranch. Junipers in places—some irrigation on the creeks. Lots of Mormon folks. Bunch of small ranchers, and plenty of stolen horses come through there."

"Why would the killers head there?"

"It's the next stop on the outlaw trail. But I know a fella I can trust up there."

"That would be good."

"Yes, in a place like that a friend can be a lifesaver. Being a Gentile and a stranger, it could be a tough country for me to learn anything. But money talks."

"How much money?"

"Aw, Lilly—ten, twenty bucks, you can get a man shot up there. It's a tough country with a cash-short society."

158

"You have any idea where they'll hide up there?"

"No, but we'll seed the place with some bribes, and I figure word will get out fast enough who we want. Those three ain't Mormons, so that will help too."

"Where haven't you been before?" She put her arms over her head and stretched with a yawn. "I'm going to go to sleep. How long till Rock Springs?"

"Be up in the night. Sleep awhile."

The warmth of the coal stove in the car made even him sleepy. But he knew he better stay awake and alert. No telling who might be on the train and recognize him. She cuddled against him and he hugged her under his arm.

Where were those three anyway? He'd hoped to rescue poor Easter before this time. That niggled him worse than anything else. There was nothing he could have done—still, his conscience kept kicking him about her plight. While he was riding the clacking rails in the swaying car, there wasn't much he could do for anyone, except to hold Lilly.

It was past midnight and dark when he checked their things with the Rock Springs depot agent. Then, with Lilly under his arm, they went up the main street for a meal and lodging. They passed several noisy saloons and dodged a drunk or two staggering down the boardwalk.

The café looked clean and the interior inviting. They ducked out of the cold night into the establishment's warmth. The rich aroma of food filled the air. It might be a good choice. The young waiter brought steaming coffee and recommended the roast elk.

They agreed on his choice of side dishes, and sat back in the booth to savor the rich coffee.

"Where will we stay tonight, Tom White?" she asked.

"I'm sure the waiter can tell us about a good hotel, Mrs. White."

They both chuckled.

Two tough-looking men came in the door and went to the counter. Slocum thought he recognized the older of the two— a man he knew as Carter. Drawing hard on his memory, he tried to think about the time and circumstances of their last meeting. Above Socorro, New Mexico. It was at the Magdalena shipping yards.

In those days, Slocum represented the Aqua Verde Land Company, and Carter had delivered some cattle with what Slocum considered the outfit's smudged brands. Andy Eager, the brand inspector, agreed, so they ran four head into the chute and shaved around the brand on each of them. It was obvious then that the Aqua Verde brand had been altered.

Carter disappeared before they could serve a warrant on him. But Slocum had no desire to renew his acquaintance—in fact, he'd rather let that dog lie considering his purpose in Rock Springs.

"You know them?" she asked in a low voice, indicating the pair.

"The one on the right's name is Carter. He's a rustler from New Mexico."

She nodded. "I understand."

The waiter delivered the food and they ate. He wondered if Carter would even recognize him, but they soon became busy eating the fine meal. The side dishes were mashed potatoes under cream gravy, green beans, sweet whole corn, brown yeast biscuits with butter.

"This is the best food we've had lately," she said between bites.

Slocum agreed, chewing the tender elk meat. "Wonderful."

"Maybe we've been eating too much of our own cooking."

"You may be right."

"Well, I'd bet Green River food is a letdown after this meal."

The two at the counter finished their pie and coffee. Carter cast a blank look at him and they left. Slocum hoped Carter had forgotten the Socorro incident. Slocum paid for their meal and they headed up the boardwalk for the Palace Hotel, which the waiter said was the best in town.

In their small hotel room at last, Slocum looked down on

the dimly lit street under their window. He wondered what the Green River country would be like this trip. All day on the train, he'd watched cloud layers move in that he felt were harbingers of a winter storm coming. It was time for one.

She came and clung to his shoulder with both hands locked over it. "You selling your thoughts?"

"For you they're free. I am concerned a new storm might be coming."

"What should we do, stay denned up in this room till spring?"

He turned and took her by the waist. "That's not a bad idea."

Forehead pressed to forehead, she wiggled her nose. "I'd much rather do it in Texas where the rooms are warmer."

"That was where I thought I was headed before the first frost."

"Uh-huh."

His mouth found hers and he gathered her in his arms as they sought each other. In seconds, their clothes fell to the floor, covers were turned back, and they fell naked on the cold sheets in a tight embrace.

She pulled the covers over him in a frenzied attempt to keep some of their body heat underneath with them. It was his entry into her that made her snuggle on her back and throw her head back with a sigh.

Braced above her, he pumped his growing erection through her gates as her heels kicked him on the back of his legs. She pulled him down, so he crushed her long breasts and they were one in the spinning cocoon. He kissed her neck, face, and mouth as their fierce lovemaking grew steamier. The walls of her well contracted and her clit grew hard enough to scar his shaft with each drive in and out.

The words escaped her lips like sighs of relief as she moaned, "Yes, yes, more. Oh, yes, more. My God—"

Then like a burst dam, he came deep inside her and pressed his hips hard against her. They collapsed on the bed.

"Texas—Wyoming—who cares," she said, slurring her words, and hugged him tight.

He raised up and looked around. "Where are we anyway?"

She pulled him back down. "You know good and well. We're in Montana."

They both laughed until they cried; then they began arousing each other all over again.

Morning came and he decided the weather might take a turn for the worse. The clouds were thickening, and more were rolling in. The temperature was about freezing, and the south wind was a harbinger of the moisture that might be on the way.

After some dickering, he bought three sound horses at the livery. A dish-faced gray for Lilly, a stout bay for his saddle horse, and a powerful Roman-nosed dun for the packhorse. He named them Gray, Bay, and Dunny, had the livery man reshoe Dunny, and paid two boys to help him bring the gear up there from the station so he and Lilly could leave at dawn the next day.

Meanwhile, Lilly had bought them some new woolen underwear for the trip, thick socks, two pairs of new gloves, and two thick wool-lined vests to wear under their jumpers. The items were laid out on the bed when he returned to the room.

She swept off his felt hat and pressed her body against him. Then she put a woolen cap on his head, leaned back and looked him over, then after a nod of approval, kissed him.

When she stopped, she asked, "You have the horses?"

"A dandy gray. I think you'll like him."

"Sounds good. The store will have our food supplies loaded in panniers when we get ready to leave in the morning."

"I guess all that's done. We better get back in bed, since we won't have much chance out there, huh?"

She closed her eyes and raised her chin. "Oh—yes."

They rode down Main Street headed south in the dim light of early morning. The horses were frisky but manageable, and he was glad to see they had that much spunk. They needed to cover thirty-five miles in a short winter day. Once clear of town, they hard-trotted the horses on the road along the Union Pacific tracks. When the road forked, they followed the hand-lettered board signs to Graham. It was a settlement he knew about on the Green River where Bud Asher had lived a few years earlier when he was on the dodge.

The day passed uneventfully until middle afternoon. Then wet flecks began falling like feathers from a plucked goose. They melted on his cheeks as he turned and gave her a worried look.

"What now, big man?" she asked.

"Better den up quick as we can. There's some willows in that streambed on the left. We can make a shelter and worse comes to worst, the horses can eat them."

As soon as they stopped, he began using a hand ax to cut the willows bigger than his finger. She stripped off the dead leaves and they soon had a pile. He peeled off bark to use as string, and began tying the sticks into mats. The whips cleaned, she joined him in the falling snowflakes and they soon had two lattices. He drove some stakes in the ground about six feet apart on both sides, and then he stood the first mat up, and she held it while he stood hers up.

With some cord to hold them in the center where they overlapped, he bowed them over and tied them so that they made a U-shaped shelter. Then he tossed one of their tarps over the frame. By then the snow was several inches deep, and she used a broom of bound willows to clear out the inside while he staked down the tarp corners. When he finished, he began to build the end-frame section so the open end was toward the east and got less wind.

Finished with his west wall, he strung a tarp over it and tied it down. She smiled as he tossed the last one over the east side and made a flap. Then, resetting his cap with a wink at her, he went and used Bay to bring in some driftwood out of the streambed along with a few small trunk parts. The deepening snow made the driftwood harder to find, but they were in piles in the dry stream and he could kick them loose of the fluffy snowflakes.

By his third trip back, she had a fire going as he chugged into camp dragging a pile of driftwood.

"I reckon this will have to do," he said, stepping down and undoing the lariat. Busy recoiling rope as she undid his latigos, he laughed. "Guess I gauged it about right."

"Yes, you did. How long will the storm last?"

"Heavens, girl, it's a wonder I got the forecast right."

They spent two nights in their "house." The sun came out on the third day and the temperature remained frozen, but it was time for them to move on. They left camp in early morning treading six inches of snow, and headed southwest through the tan sandstone formations worn smooth by wind and dust. He was glad to be on the move again.

In late afternoon, a streak of wood smoke from a chimney made him nod to her. "Hope Bud Asher is still there."

"So do I." She wrapped the blanket tighter around her as she rode the gray up beside him.

They crossed the wide valley, reining up before the low-wall cabin.

"Anyone home?" Slocum shouted.

"Naw," a whisker-faced man said from the doorway and spit out on the snow. "Well, I'll be jiggered. That you, Slocum?"

He stepped off Bay. "You ain't lost your eyesight. How've you been?"

"No, and you sure ain't lost yours. Howdy, ma'am. You excuse us old hawgs. We ain't laid eyes on each other in a spell."

"No problem," she said, and laughed while dismounting. She looked around, and Slocum pointed to the outhouse.

She nodded and headed that way.

"You come right inside," Bud shouted after Lilly as he pounded Slocum on the back. "My Lord, she's a looker."

"Some breeds and a black murdered her husband."

"Ah, hell. Come on in, it's a damn sight warmer in there." Bud hustled him into the cabin. "She'll come along, huh?"

"Yes, she's tough."

"Who kilt her man?"

"A breed named Red Dog, another named Snake, and a black called Tar Boy."

"Tar Boy, huh? He got a couple of squaws with him?" Bud asked, squeezing his beard.

"Yes." Slocum turned from heating his hands at the fireplace when Lilly came inside.

"Make yourself at home, darling," Bud said to her.

"Thanks, I will." She stomped her boots on the old rug mat.

Slocum looked over at Bud. "He could have some Indian women with him. He around here?"

Bud narrowed his left eye and nodded. "Less than three miles from here in a shack."

Slocum met Lilly's questioning look and pursed his lips tight. Their chase might soon be over.

22

Red Dog had crossed the Union Pacific tracks and was headed south across the snow-covered country. He was in the Green River country. The rows of bare cottonwoods running down the valley told him so. He noticed some smoke, and knew from the ache in his hip and right leg another storm was coming in. Against the glare, he spotted an outfit—cabin, corrals, and small buildings.

He'd need to be careful approaching the place. If she was a Morman widow, he'd be fine, but there were some tough people lived in this country besides them. Homesteaders were dumb farmers, lambs to prey on. The others were tough. Like him, they were eking a living out of this hard land that had little to give them.

He decided to ride up to the place and act like he could pay for his meal and lodging. That worked as a decoy. Most of these white women, with the prospect of even a little cash money, would feed a traveler, even a breed. Maybe make him stay outside, him being a savage. That was why he'd kilt them honyockers up there in Wyoming—they wanted him to stay outside. Too good to let him come inside their dirt-floored shack. Injuns lived better in tepees with skins on the floor. Who did they think they were anyway?

The stock dogs barked and danced around. He dismounted, and at last the board door opened a crack.

"What do you want?" a woman's voice asked.

"I'm hungry. I have not eaten in two days. I have some money. I can pay you."

"My husband will be back soon."

He knew the *soon* part was a lie. He'd heard the tremble in her voice that betrayed her. "All I want is some food. I have some silver coins."

"No . . . I can't help you. I'm sorry."

"How far is it to town?" he asked, knowing well there was only a store, saloon, and blacksmith at Graham farther downstream according to what the old man the day before told him.

"Not far. Go south—you—you can find it—they'll sell you food."

By the tone of her voice, he knew she wasn't an old woman. "I'm weak," he said. He rubbed his stomach. "I haven't eaten anything in days."

"Not my problem, you ride on. He'll be here soon."

"I'd give you a silver dollar for some food." His gaze set on the weathered gray board on the door. He hoped his offer was high enough. What did she look like?

"They will feed you."

"Lady, I'm starving—" He buckled his knees and fell on the ground.

One of the collies came over and licked his face. *Get away.* But he dared not move.

"Oh—" she said, and wrapping a blanket around her, she rushed out to see about him. "Get back," she said to the collie.

Dog barely opened an eye to see an attractive woman looking down at him. His hand shot out and caught her arm in a viselike grip.

A choked-off scream hung in her throat.

"Don't say a word," he said through his teeth and sprang to his feet, jerking her up and twisting her around and toward the house. The two surprised dogs yelped and dodged away. "You want these two dogs alive, don't say a word."

No way he wanted them upset. They acted suspicious, but it was only a few feet to the open doorway. He roughly shoved her toward it and in seconds, they were inside the warm room. With his back against the door as he watched her like a hawk watches his prey, she backed away in shocked fear.

"Who—who are you?"

"I am a man. I am not a dog. You were going to treat me like a dog."

"No. No, I wasn't. I swear." She collapsed on a chair, looking like a cornered animal with no place to run. Her reddish curls fell over her eyes and she swept them back, but the curls kept falling.

"I better show you I am a man," he said, anger coursing through his veins. He ripped open his pants.

"Nooo," she said, and looked away. "I know you're a man."

He stepped over to her, grasped a handful of her hair to force her to look at the limp dick in his hand. "You see this?"

When she didn't answer him, he shook her.

"Yes. Yes—you're a man." She tried to pry his hold loose with her fingers, but she was no match for him and he only hurt her more for trying.

"Where is your husband?" He reinforced his question with a jerk.

"Salt Lake—"

"Then I could have starved out there? Right?"

"Yes, yes. Please, please, don't pull anymore. I'll tell you all—all you want to know." Her eyelashes were wet with tears.

"Good." He released her hair. "Get up and fix me some food."

"What?" she asked, trying to sweep her hair back from her face.

"What do you have?"

"Some ham? Some rice? Some beans?" She turned up her palms.

"Ham, biscuits, gravy, and rice." She was in her early twenties by his calculation. Had a willowy figure, not skinny like the last one. Why was she out there? Mormons usually put their older wives that were barren out on these isolated ranches, not young ones like her. The one Snake killed and mutilated was in her thirties. No kids with her either.

Woodenly, she nodded at him. "I'll fix it for you."

"Good," he said as he put his dick away and buttoned his pants. He'd sure need it later. The notion kinda warmed him. He took off his coat and hat, hung them on a peg as she busied herself getting food ready while from time to time cutting worried looks at him. On a whim, he opened the door and saw the two horses standing hangdogged in the falling snow. After supper, he'd tie her up and then put them up. For some reason, he didn't trust her.

This might be a good place to weather out the storm. Not bad, not bad at all, he decided, watching the sway of her hips and body movements as she prepared the food.

"What is your name?" she asked, not looking at him.

"Red."

She nodded. "Mine is Loretta."

"Loretta who?" All white people had last names. He held his hands toward the blazing logs in the fireplace. The heat felt good penetrating his skin.

"Loretta Furman."

"What wife number are you?"

"Three," she said in a small voice.

"How many he got now?"

She shook her head. "He doesn't tell me since he brought me up here."

"How long ago did he drag you up here?" Sitting on one of the ladder-back chairs, he leaned on his knees and watched her cook. Not hard to imagine what her body under the simple dress looked like.

"Two years ago, three months, and two weeks."

Her words amused him enough. He grinned at her. She saw being there like a prison sentence. Just like those prisoners did in that Nebraska jail he'd once sat in. "You like it up here?"

"No. There's no church up here. No women to talk to. My daughters are in Salt Lake with some of the other *sisters*."

"How many daughters you have?"

"Two—all the children I had." She turned up her hands and shook her head, close to tears. "I miss not seeing them grow up."

"Do you wish to leave here?"

She shook her head and looked up shocked. "I am a married woman."

He nodded.

"Why are you here?" she asked.

"Two men I trusted stole my money. I sold a ranch," he lied. "Then they robbed me of all the money."

"Who are they?" She removed the Dutch oven with a hook to the flat rocks in front of the fireplace and rotated the lid. Then she set it back.

"A breed called Snake and a black calls himself Tar Boy."

She shook her head, indicating that they were unknown to her. "Are they around here?"

"I'm not sure. But I think they may try to hide here."

"They won't be hard to find. I mean, a black man. How much money did they steal?"

"Thousands."

"You must have had a big ranch."

"Yes, it was a big ranch in Montana."

"What will you do with the money?"

"Go someplace where it never snows, like St. David in Arizona Territory." He waited for her reaction to the name of this Mormon town.

"They say it is very hot and dry there."

"You have people live there?" Maybe she would want to go there—with him.

She nodded. "My best friend lives there."

"Is she happy—" The dogs were barking and he drew his six-gun. "Who is out there?"

"I don't know. I wasn't expecting anyone." She looked upset.

They had already seen his horses. It was near dark. "Invite them in," he said.

"But why—"

He could hear someone shouting above the dogs barking. "Do as I say."

Loretta nodded and, skirt in hand, rushed to the door. It was unbarred. She opened it and spoke. "Who's out there?"

"Josh Butler, RT outfit—ma'am, my horse went lame and I wondered if I could borrow one of yours. I'll bring him back—this snow is getting thick."

"Know him?" Dog hissed.

Loretta shook her head. "Must be a new hand."

"Invite him in."

A frown of disapproval creased her smooth forehead. "He can take a horse and go—"

"No. He'll warn them that I am here."

"Come in," she said. "Lands, it is snowing hard."

The cowboy came toward the house though Dog could not see him. She stepped back for him to enter.

"I didn't mean to bother you," he said. "I guess your husband rode in—"

"Hands in the air," Dog ordered.

"Wh-what? I didn't mean nothing. My horse is lame and I just wanted to borrow—"

"Shut up," Dog said, and shoved him to a chair. "Get some rope."

Loretta obeyed. Dog took his pistol and stuck it in his waistband. Then he tied the stuttering cowboy's hands behind his back.

"What's g-going on here?" he asked.

Next, Dog bound his feet and secured him to the chair. "I'm looking for a black man stole all my money."

"I seed one in G-Graham yesterday."

"What did he look like?"

His prisoner shrugged. "They all look alike."

"What's your name?"

"J-Josh Nutler. I mean Butler."

"He tall?"

"Very tall."

"What was he doing?"

"Getting supplies for them squaws of his at the store. He's pretty rich. Got lots of money to spend."

"He's spending my money. He stole it from me." Red-faced, Dog slammed his fist on the table. "That's my money."

"Oh—"

"Where's he at now?"

"Some cabin west of town."

"You ever been there?"

"No. But he hadn't ought to be hard to find. Cut me loose and I'll take you there."

"Supper's on," Loretta said, and began putting the food on the table.

Dog nodded to her. Somehow, all this business about his money and that black sumbitch freely spending it had shut down his appetite.

"We'll see," he told his prisoner,

The salty ham had been smoked and tasted fine. Her biscuits were hot in his fingers. So he let them cool while he reached for the butter.

"Where you from?" Dog asked his prisoner as he ate the good food. "Before you came here?"

"Cedar City."

Loretta sat across from the prisoner. Dog was between them on the end. He chewed on a bite of hot biscuit, then pointed at him.

"You and her having an affair?"

They both blinked at him in disbelief.

"Too convenient. You said you didn't know her husband would be here." He turned to Loretta. "You said you didn't know him. Hell, you two been having sex."

"No," she screamed, and reached out to cut him with a butcher knife.

Dog spilled over backward in his chair and tried to draw his six-gun in a tangle of his chair and his legs. Before he could get the .44 clear of his holster, she busted him over the head with a rolling pin and the lights went out.

23

Lilly was up and making coffee. The aroma of Bud's pipe tobacco filled the room. When Slocum threw his legs over the
side of the rope bed, he rubbed his dry eyes. The recharged
fireplace was driving the cold out of the one-room cabin.

"Another day," Bud said, and pointed his pipe at Lilly.
"This lady friend of yours ain't no stranger to cooking either."

She smiled at them, busy making biscuits.

With his calloused hand, Slocum rubbed the back of his
own neck. "She's been spoiling me."

"If'n it was in the old days, I'd try and buy her."

"You bought a wife?" she asked, and frowned at Bud.

"Bought several."

"They were Indian women," Slocum said.

"They were wives," Bud said, and used his black pipe
stem to emphasize his words. "When I was a young buck, I
had me a Ute woman. Taught me more about medicines in
plants than a doctor knew."

"She was older'n you as I recall you saying," Slocum put
in, pulling on his pants.

Bud laughed. "Yeah, she was. Probably twice my age
then. But she was smart—good-looking too. Hell, I was in
love with her."

"What happened to her?" Lilly asked, greasing the Dutch oven for the biscuits.

"Couple of Arapaho bucks kilt her in a raid."

Lilly winced.

"I had others, but not a one was smart as she was."

"You were a mountain man?"

"Naw, Lilly, I come too late fur that. Just lived off trapping, hiring out to kill wolves and varmints. I was more Injun than white in them days."

"Bud ran away from home when he was eleven."

"That young?" She looked surprised.

"My old man beat me hard one night, and I figured he either wanted me gone or dead. So I up and left. Wasn't no worse being on me own than there."

"Never saw any relatives again?"

"No." He relit his pipe and made sucking sounds rebuilding the fire in the bowl.

"Why live here?" She put the lid on the Dutch oven with a clank, then shoveled red-hot ashes on top.

"I'm like Slocum. I look over my shoulder a lot. Not so bad anymore. Two or three of them fellars that was after me have gone to the hereafter." His cackling laughter sounded bright.

She straightened and then nodded that she understood.

"Well, you done heard my story, what's yours?" Bud asked her.

"When I was eighteen, I married Josh McCullem and we left Fort Worth the next day for his ranch, as he called it. Our first house was made of posts with a grass roof and a cowhide door. On my twenty-fourth birthday, he moved me into a large hacienda with his cattle-drive money. I have a fine home. If you ever get by there, stop and stay."

"How in the blue blazes did you get up here?"

"We were going home from driving a large herd of cattle to Montana. Josh and his foreman wanted to stop and hunt for elk in the Big Horns. They were murdered, and since then Slocum has been my guide tracking his killers."

"What'll you do after today?"

"Oh, you mean after we catch the killers? I guess go home and run the ranch."

"Yes, after we rouse them out of their hole," Bud answered.

"You going along?" Slocum asked him.

"I wouldn't miss it for nothing. I got old Betsy oiled and ready. Figure a man can always use a good Spencer rifle backing him up." Bud bent over in a deep coughing spell, until at last he wiped his mouth on a kerchief and shook his head. "Unless you don't want me."

"We may need an army." Slocum accepted fresh coffee in a tin cup from Lilly.

"I doubt that," she said.

They left in the new snow that fell the evening before. The packhorse Dunny whined after them from the corral. He didn't like being left behind, Slocum figured. They reached Graham two hours later and reined up at the store. The sun was melting the snow off the porch roof and water was dripping off the edge.

Bud nodded, and said he'd go in and find out about the location of the cabin where he thought Tar Boy was staying. Slocum looked around. He could smell the coal smoke coming from the log shed that served as the blacksmith shop. Across the street, the saloon appeared to still be closed.

In a few minutes, Bud came out with a fistful of peppermint candy sticks and gave two to Lilly and two to Slocum. "It's about three miles west on that mountain."

Slocum nodded and started to rein Bay around. A man in an apron came out on the porch and acknowledged them.

"That's Joseph Smith Martin," Bud said.

"Mrs. McCullem, and my name's Slocum," Slocum said.

"Good day, ma'am. You're welcome to stay here."

"Thanks," she said. "I've rode this far, I'll go with them."

"He was alone when he came here?" Slocum asked.

"Yes," Martin said, "but he had two Injun women stayed with the horses." They turned as a rider came in with what looked like a body over a second horse.

"That's Josh Butler of the RT outfit," Martin said with a frown. "Wonder what he's got."

The fresh-faced puncher reined up and nodded to everyone. "This breed back here tried to rustle my horse last night. Figured I better bring his carcass in."

"You shoot him?" Martin asked with a frown.

The cowboy nodded. "Me or him, I figured."

"Mind if we look at him?" Slocum asked.

"I don't care."

He and Bud took the body off the horse and laid it on the ground. They unwrapped it without a word. One look at the dark face and Slocum knew it was Red Dog. He nodded to Bud and did the same to Lilly.

"You were lucky," Slocum said to Butler. "He killed her husband. Was there anyone with him?"

"No. Is there another?"

"Two more. The one we can't place is a breed like him, only with a darker complexion and a sharper face."

"This one was leading a white horse and saddle, but wasn't no other I could see."

"That sounded like his partner Snake's horse all right." Slocum wished he had more information. Were both breeds dead? He might never learn.

"I'll make you a check for the reward I offered," Lilly said, and dismounted.

Butler swept off his hat, looking taken aback. "I figured he was bad, but I never expected a reward, ma'am."

"Turned out to be your day," Slocum said, still thinking about the riderless white horse. Had Snake got himself killed? He glanced at the mountain. Tar Boy was still up there on his guard.

With a pencil, she made out a check to Butler on her saddle seat and handed it to him.

"Why, that's ten months' wages—" He blinked in disbelief at her, and then back at the check.

"What you going to do with it?" Martin asked.

"Leave this country. I've got me a gal in mind." He waved the check. "I may try my luck with her in a warmer climate."

"Good luck," Lilly said.

'Oh, one more thing," Slocum said. "You've got to worry about planting him too."

"I can handle it."

"Good," Slocum said, and then looked at the other two. "Mount up. Daylight's burning."

"Yes, Mr. Boss," she said, and smiled with a wink at Bud.

They followed the untracked ruts under the snow, headed uphill through the juniper, and soon reached the pines. In an hour, Slocum could see a column of smoke and held up his hand.

"From here on we need to be extra careful. He might be real on edge without those other two."

"I can skirt the mountain and come in from the north," Bud said, waving his Spencer in that direction.

"Good. We can give you a while to get around there."

"You can go up closer. There is a basin, a meadow this side of the cabin. I figure you can stay in the timber on this side out of sight up there."

"See you in a while," Lilly said.

"Durn right, girl," Bud said, and headed north through the pines.

She pushed the goatskin gloves down on her fingers. "I'm glad this is about over. But I can't say I want to part with you."

He nodded as they pushed up to the rim of the flats. "Shooting starts, you take cover."

"I understand. You wouldn't consider being Tom White and running my ranch?"

"Lilly, your offer makes me want to try. But I'm a realist. They'd come for me. Slip of a lip in some bar. 'I seen Slocum.' They'd come."

"Oh, Slocum—"

He put his fingers to his mouth to silence her. Across on the far side of the meadow, a woman was running from the trees. Her fringe waved as she flew over a post-rail fence and started toward them.

"Who is she?"

He jerked out his Winchester and levered in a cartridge. "Her name's Easter."

"The woman from the cabin?"

"That's her."

Dismounted, he used a tree to rest the rifle against as he watched her run as hard as she could, looking back from time to time.

"Tell me if you see anyone coming after her." He resumed sighting down the rifle barrel.

He could hear Easter's heavy breathing as Lilly went to the edge of the trees and waved Easter toward them. She about collapsed on her knees when she saw Slocum.

"He's got traps set for you," she said, out of breath, and collapsed on the snow. Lilly comforted her as Slocum nodded and went for his horse.

"Be careful," Easter said after him, still out of breath.

He paused. "Red Dog is dead."

She nodded. "Snake went to stop him."

Slocum nodded. "He must have killed Snake then." He raised his gaze to the smoke column. "Who else is over there?"

"Mia."

"Red Dog's woman?"

"Yes. She's with Tar Boy."

Slocum booted Bay out in the meadow and short-loped him for the gate in the fence. He looked all around before he dismounted and shoved the bars aside. The skin on his neck itched when he remounted and set the Bay on up the path.

In sight of the cabin, he stepped down and left Bay ground-tied. Nothing moved at the cabin. He took off his right glove, shed his jumper, and hung it on the saddle horn. In case he needed to move fast, the coat would only hinder him.

He advanced, using a shed first to shelter him in case Tar Boy stepped out to shoot at him. The cabin door remained unopened. At last he reached an outhouse, and could see the cabin door from the side of the structure.

"Tar Boy! Throw out your gun and come out," he shouted.

"That be you, Tom White?"

"It's me."

"Red Dog always said we should have kilt yeah."

"He's dead. A puncher killed him yesterday trying to steal his horse."

"Snake?"

"I think Red Dog killed him. That puncher said Dog was leading a white horse with an empty saddle."

"Sumbitch was like a weasel."

"He was. Throw out your gun and come out."

"What fur? They going hang me sure as shit, ain't they?"

"Be a trial."

"Now what chance a black man have at a Wyoming trial?" Tar Boy laughed.

"I ain't the law."

"What you say I give you all this money and I go on my way?"

"That's Mrs. McCullem's money."

"You could give it to her and she'd never know."

"I ain't cutting no deals." Overhead, a magpie landed in a pine bough and the snowflakes fell in a shower. The wet snow dampened Slocum's face while filtering by.

"I figured we done killed you that night. But you got away. My, my, Tom White, you done living a second life now, maybe more."

"Time's up, Tar Boy."

The door burst open and Slocum saw the smoke coming from a rifle muzzle as the black man's large form filled the doorway. Slocum took aim, and his first bullet made Tar Boy hesitate in his stride and drop the rifle. Shot number two made him flinch again as he fought to draw his pistol. The third round buckled his knees, and Tar Boy sprawled face-down in the snow.

Slocum let the rifle down and exhaled. He looked up in time to Mia aiming at him. Then a shot rang out and she dropped the rifle. Hit hard, she slowly sank to the ground. Her rifle rattled, striking the ground ahead of her.

At the corner of the cabin, Bud sat his pony and the smoking rifle butt was still on his shoulder.

"That's all of them," Slocum said, and nodded at Bud. "Thanks."

Slocum crossed the yard and kicked away the handgun in Tar Boy's grip. Then he stepped over Mia's crumpled form, and the first thing he saw on the table inside were piles of gold coins. Even in the shadowy cabin, they shone.

"Life's pretty cheap. Ain't it?" Bud said, coming in after him.

"Pretty damn cheap. They should have figured they'd never get away with it."

"Sounded like to me they never counted on you."

"They made that mistake twice," he said, looking up as the two women came around Mia's corpse and stopped in the doorway.

"What's that?" Lilly asked.

"I guess this is what's left of your money."

"Thank you. Help me find a sack," Lilly said to Easter.

Slocum nodded as they began to collect the coins, and he went to the doorway to gaze out at the countryside. Maybe he could go on to San Antonio now?

24

Slocum wore a white shirt, a tie, a brown suit, and a snowy white ten-gallon hat. His handmade boots shuffled to the guitar polka music as he swept Lilly around the dance floor. Her head thrown back, she laughed at his comments about how cold it would be in Wyoming. The music stopped and they joined the others at the bar.

Her friends, area ranchers and business folks, were glad to have her home safe. They had accepted Slocum as one of them. The Bar M Ranch was back to working in full swing, and Slocum was enjoying the fandango.

"What did Bud say that cowboy did with the money you paid him?" he asked her, leaning on the bar.

"Said he got someone's wife and took her away with him to Arizona."

"Sounds like he knew what he wanted to do. But you can't kid me. Easter wrote the letter. Bud couldn't write his name that good."

"How many wives does that make him?"

Slocum winked at her. "I've lost count. Let's dance."

"Certain—what's Curly want? Something must be wrong."

Slocum and Lilly went to the edge of the dance floor where the ranch foreman waited. The shorter man was shifting his weight from one foot to the other.

"What's wrong?"

"Tom, them two fellas you warned me about showed up at the ranch this evening. One was riding a big Appaloosa horse like you said." He lowered his voice. "Said they was Kansas deputies and they'd be back when you got home tomorrow."

Slocum turned and saw the paleness of Lilly's face. He nodded.

"What will you—" she gasped.

"Thanks, Curly. Take care of things." He shook the man's hand. "You can run her. Take good care of Lilly."

"Oh, yes, sir."

When Curly left, he guided Lilly behind the drapes. In the darkness, he took her tall willowy form in his arms and kissed her long and hard.

Then he swept the hair from her face. "The time has come."

She nested her face against his shoulder. "God be with you."

An hour later, Slocum looked out of the open boxcar door as the freight chugged along at fifteen miles an hour away from San Antonio. The candle lamps made orange squares in the adobe hovel windows along the tracks, and the train engine whistled in the night.

He'd be a while getting over her.

Watch for

SLOCUM AND THE KILLERS

350th novel in the exciting SLOCUM series
from Jove

Coming in April!

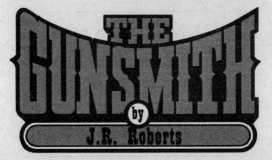

GIANT-SIZED ADVENTURE FROM AVENGING ANGEL LONGARM.

BY TABOR EVANS

2006 GIANT EDITION

LONGARM AND THE OUTLAW EMPRESS
978-0-515-14235-8

2007 GIANT EDITION

LONGARM AND THE GOLDEN EAGLE SHOOT-OUT
978-0-515-14358-4

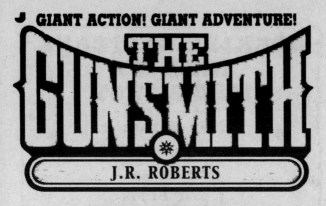

penguin.com

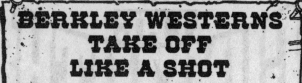

BERKLEY WESTERNS TAKE OFF LIKE A SHOT

Lyle Brandt

Peter Brandvold

Jack Ballas

J. Lee Butts

Jory Sherman

Ed Gorman

Mike Jameson

Don't miss the best Westerns from Berkley.